I Lied For You

Brie Owen Mystery Series, Volume 1

Zee David

Published by Eddy2wice, 2022.

This is a work of fiction. Similarities to real people, places, or events are entirely coincidental.

I LIED FOR YOU

First edition. October 16, 2022.

Written by Zee David.

To you, who your fingers are, sweeping through this page.

I write because you read.

Without a reason, there is no essence.

Thank you for grabbing my work!

Enjoy

What's your wish?

A whistle echoed into the night.
The tune he hummed traveled into an open space.
Her screams and cries, him—adamant.
Drenched in her blood, the sky cried.
Thunder lodged fear in her mind.
His justice must be done.
His conviction: He was a genie.
He granted her a wish.
She pleaded for her life,
His belief: He saved her.
She yelled for help.
The rue flower: his symbol of indignation.

CHAPTER ONE

Brie

A single thunder strike, straight from the night, resided in the most emotional part of my brain. It was strange that the simple noise could rouse me from bed, even though I was in a deep trance. In a country like Monthel, June was the rainy season, and a clasp of thunder followed, but it still shocked me from sleep.

I got up and assembled my tired legs. The storm's impact on my being was nerving. Getting back in bed soon wasn't happening. I walked towards the windows, closing them shut. Less than a second later, the wind guided the rain in that direction, spraying the barred window with water droplets. At least my waking up was not in vain.

I stood at the window for a while, deciding to peer through the darkness and see what it held onto the other side. My dampened neck and shivering hands reminded me of the dream I had before the interruption. I still thought about that day. The memory refused to leave, gloating in its ability to taunt me.

A vivid image of her darkened eyes, with tears dripping down her face. Her palms were cold and blue as I stumbled over them. My feet stuck as if someone had glued them to the brown clay soil, and his hand clenched to my collar. My eyes blurred, and my throat tightened. I couldn't breathe. It played out in my dreams that day.

MARCH 8TH, 2007, DENTON Falls

I had everything planned out. My parents wouldn't allow me out of the house without a decent excuse and, of course, a strong alibi. So, I created one.

Eve was a dear friend, the very best. She wanted me to spend the night at her place and do all the stuff 12-year-old girls loved getting immersed in. I was excited to hang out with her, eager for what would follow.

We had a good time, or rather, I observed Eve have fun. She looked genuinely happy and satisfied, her eyes were like the morning sun. She fell asleep almost immediately after her head hit the pillow, exhaustion taking its toll on her fragile frame. The big red clock was next to the reading table, counting along with the timer. I might have dozed off, I guess I did, because the next time I checked the clock, it was already a few minutes past five.

I raced out of the house, careful not to wake my friend, the pesky guard. My knees ached as I reached the top of the hills, tired of being dragged about in fatigue. I compelled them to keep moving, aware that I had to return before Eve or her parents got up.

A snap sound from the twig of a tree pressed under my foot caused my heart to jump. And even to my disbelief, I ran down these woods by myself.

"Gabriella," a breathy voice called into the distance.

I turned back for a second, catching a quick glimpse of her trying to catch up with me, her long black hair all over the place as it got tossed by the wind. The plowing sound of her feet against the soil.

"I thought, she was asleep". I rolled my eyes

"Wait for me!" she pleaded, but my racing heart gave my feet the strength to jump up the hill faster, blood pumping with each stride.

"Hurry!" I motioned to Eve with my hand while the wintry morning breeze brushed against my skin.

From a distance, the chirping sound of birds. They seemed to gather around us, celebrating our small feat of leaving the house undetected. I patted myself on the shoulder.

"Ga-Gabriella, why are we going this far into the woods?" She panted while she spoke. I turned around, chuckling as Eve placed her hand on her knees. "My mum might realize that we snuck out of the house." Her voice was low and shaky.

"We? I didn't ask you to come with me," I whispered.

"Well, I wouldn't allow you to run out by yourself without a clue where you were going," she replied. Why did she think I did not know where I was heading to? I tucked a strand of my hair behind my ear.

"Then follow me. In silence." I motioned.

"Let's just go back, Gabriella," Eve pleaded softly.

"You are no fun, Eve," I snapped at her as I climbed up the hill once again. "You can return whenever you want to."

"So, who are you meeting in the woods this early?" she asked, resigned to the knowledge that I wouldn't change my mind.

"Hurry!" I yelled again, deciding not to answer her question.

"Gabriella!"

Silence.

"Gabriella!"

Silence.

"Gabriella!" Her voice buzzed in my ears like a persistent bee. I imagined her suddenly turning into a bird and making her way for my palms. As she whispered, I imagined swatting at her tiny form.

I giggled silently at that thought, earning a stern look from Eve's big, brown eyes.

Ecstasy setting in, I hummed in delight as we continued our brief journey. I couldn't wait for a second to reach the little hut in the woods. My heart raced at the thought of seeing him again. Although we met recently, I had an irreparable crush on him. Sean was two years older than me, and even though my mum wouldn't cease giving me lectures about staying away from him, her warning fell on deaf ears. I was going to meet Sean anyway, which was why I pretended to have a sleepover with Eve.

"Hurry up, Eve. Why are you so far behind?"

Her long, untied hair wisped with the morning wind. "Can't you see I'm trying?" She stopped before replying, her two arms placed against her knees. "You are too fast. Why are we going into the woods to meet him?" she asked inquisitively.

"Who said it was a 'him'?" I asked, not exactly enthusiastic about the idea of her meeting Sean.

"Well, is it?"

I shrugged my shoulders and rolled my eyes at her question. "Just hurry."

As I waited for Eve to catch up, I looked around, taking in the calm and wistful ambiance nature never failed to bring. The rue flowers bloomed bluish green with yellowish shades, their beauty and innocence filling the air with their exquisite scent. The beautiful petals of the Ruta flowers aligning with the aura of sunrise looked even more peaceful in their habitat. Were they called Ruta? I thought that was what Sean called them the last time I was here as he tried showing me around. That meeting was sadly cut short, as I had to leave before my mum noticed I was gone.

I looked behind, wondering why Eve hadn't caught up with me yet. I was greeted with the hilarious sight of her face bellowed to the ground and her long hair flowing behind her back. Eve was never a strong type, but sometimes I wished she was.

I walked back to meet her, going down on my knees. "We're almost there, Eve. Just one more push." She smiled, lifting her hands into the air like I had given her the energy to catch up with me. I could hear her light-hearted laugh echoing through the woods and traveling over the wind.

"Race me!" I screamed excitedly, taking off with Eve behind me.

"Wait for me, Gabriella." She laughed, her hand raised in the air and her dimples on full display as she tried to catch up. I silently hoped he wouldn't find her dimples more attractive than mine.

"You are too slow, Eve. Remember, we have to get back before anyone notices we are gone." I jumped over a log of wood that had fallen onto the path from the heavy downpour the previous night, waiting to help Eve climb over it too.

"Well, I'm trying," Eve responded, her laugh echoing through the woods again.

"Shhh... you are going to scare the birds away." I gestured with one of my slender fingers placed on my lips.

My nightmares always ended there, leaving my brain with enough time to conjure up the remaining pieces of what had happened that day. It had been fifteen years, but I still remembered every detail. The chill I felt as a strange face greeted me from the hut where Sean and I always met. I still remembered the way he glared at me, how the colour of the sun's rays became one with the hate his red eyes held. I had been too scared to call out for Sean, afraid still to look out for Eve. I was shivering, looking around myself. It was better than staring into those dreadful eyes.

As if on cue, the man had broken the silence, his voice sending chills through my back.

"Hello, Gabriella. What do you wish for?"

I dragged my brain to the present. I distracted myself with the TV and a warm glass of milk, settling into the squashy couch and draping a nearby quilt over my goose-bumped legs. The quilt, with fern-like leaves and small, green, yellowish petals, its edges decorated with frills, had been an anonymous birthday present. I had no intention of using it until the seasons shifted, bringing frigid temperatures.

The news was on, and the camera was focused on the face of a weeping mother. She was covered with blotches and a runny nose. "There is still no update on a suspect for the recently murdered girls," the reporter said in a mechanical voice. "But all hands are on deck, and the perpetrator of this gruesome act will be brought to book."

I stayed still for a moment, scared that if I breathed too hard, it would be my mother crying there in front of the camera, that it would be me lying in the pool of blood, with that face lighting up in glee above me.

My phone rang, jerking me out of the short but fear-filled trance. I knew it was my editor-in-chief before I picked up the call. She was the only one who usually called at this hour.

"Did I wake you?" Clarissa asked.

"You know I barely sleep these days." I put my hands through my untidy auburn hair, mentally booking an appointment with the hairstylist.

"Don't we all?" she said, chuckling softly. "Now, the reason I'm calling you, Brie, is because you need to interview a witness. I'm assuming you have seen the news?" she spoke gravely.

I changed my name to Brie after the incident fifteen years ago. And everyone now called me that, including my mum.

"I just did, grisly and most undignified."

The third girl was found in the fetal position, and a rue flower was left beside her, read the title on the screen as the distraught mother wept loudly. I thought of a poem by Jay Neugeboren, "An Orphan's Tale."

A wife who loses a husband is called a widow.
A husband who loses a wife is called a widower.
A child who loses his parents is called an orphan.
There is no word for a parent who loses a child.
That's how awful the loss is.

I turned it off instantly, unwilling to be plunged back into something I tried so hard to forget. "I have arranged for you to meet up with this witness by six a.m. So, I advise you to start getting ready." My boss continued, "I want this to happen before the other reporters swing by."

"I will be there."

"And please, Brie, tidy up your hair."

I laughed as I clicked off the call. Clarissa knew how to put me in a better mood. I ran into the bathroom to begin my morning ritual, spending more time on my stubborn hair. I got it from my mum, and she got it from hers. I wish the generational hereditary gene had skipped me. At least I wouldn't be stuck trying to tame hair with no plans to listen to me. No amount of brushing made it sleek unless I visited a hair salon.

I plugged in my hot iron, firmly patting my hair strands and letting the hot iron through them. This was annoying. I scarcely had time to fix my stubborn hair.

I took a glimpse at my cellphone, afraid I would be late to meet the witness in thirty minutes. That's when my phone rang. "It's Brie on the line," I answered, half expecting it to be my boss again, reminding me not to be late and to take good care of my hair.

Silence.

"Hello?"

"Hello, Gabriella. What do you wish for?"

My brown eyes were cloudy, the strength of my calloused hand so weak that I could feel my phone fall out of my hand. An image of myself in the mirror, half ragged hair with grey smoke from one of my hair strands.

I threw my hot iron carelessly into the bathroom sink. He called me Gabriella, the name that felt eerily familiar yet like a distant memory. No one had called me by that name, not after I moved away from Denton Falls, my hometown, where my life was wrapped in that misfortune.

CHAPTER TWO

Brie

I turned on the faucet and let the hot water pour down my skin. The pain from the scorching water felt good over my skin. The calluses from the past were not yet gone.

His voice was a reminder of the detective from fifteen years ago—the one who saw through me. I hated her resilience. She was a nemesis to my being.

His voice, like debris after an earthquake, still resonated over my skin. I looked over my mirror, foggy like my brain. I had to stop whatever I was doing and head out to see the witness, but my senses weren't responding to my will.

I looked in my mirror. My reflection was gone, and in the mirror was a young girl. She looked sad. In her hand was a teddy bear she clutched tightly.

I was now in a trance, my body plunged into the woods with the girl. A dark and cold swamp with tall trees. She wore a white nightgown, with her wavy hair pulled into a bun.

"What are you doing here?" I asked. Though she didn't reply. She cried, rubbing her eyes with her palm; then said, "Daddy, I'm sorry."

"Why are you sorry?" My words held into thin air, and a chilly wind brushed over my skin. The night became foggy. Suddenly I couldn't see the girl. Silence filled the air, and then came a loud giggle.

"Wait for me, Eve," the little girl said. I looked around, and the fog was gone. In front of me were two girls. The first girl and the girl named Eve — unsettlingly matching my friend's name—stood closely.

Her friend wore a pleated red and white dress like my friend's on the night of the sleepover. She had her hair braided into a ponytail.

I had to get someone to help them. The woods were dangerous for two young girls.

"Where are you girls going?" I asked, but both girls giggled. "Race me, Eve," the girl said. "You are too weak, and I hate you for it."

I patted my back pocket but didn't have my phone on me. An older boy approached both girls, and looking directly at me, placed his finger over his lips.

"Shhh."

Then he pointed towards a hut, one I hadn't seen before. The girls fastened their paces and raced into the hut. I followed inside a bright hut with brown wooden floors and a small window; on its wall was a deer's head. On the couch, an embroidered cloth of flowers, weirdly similar to my quilt.

I heard a humming voice, a lullaby. I slowly turned and saw a tall, thin woman. As hard as I tried to understand the image in front of my eyes, I couldn't make up for what she was doing. It was like she didn't notice the girls walk in.

A strong, mildew scent filled the air. She stirred something, something in a pot–a horrid smell.

"Girls," I said. "This is trespassing. She might see you."

A clanking sound from a silver spoon, and the girls were no longer giggling. I was no longer in the hut but in a room with a tile floor.

The room was dark, and above another girl, who seemed to me an older self of the young girl, was a blinking bulb. It was me. It had been me this whole time. I watched myself panic as an older woman appeared in a black uniform. The tag on her breast pocket read: Anita Zac. Her stern voice filled the room.

"I'm not buying this, Gabriella. What happened?"

Her high-pitched voice pulled me away from the room, and I jerked back to consciousness. My eyes panned around the white-painted wall with triangular tiles. The mirror was still foggy. I wiped it, the trance still vivid. A visit from my nemesis. What happened? Did I fall asleep in these few minutes? Why was the scenery so surreal?

The hairs on my neck felt prickly.

I will be late to meet the witness.

CHAPTER THREE

Detective Anita

The buzzing sound of cars and the lively vibe of this city mesmerized me every time I walked around it.

Today was supposed to be one of those days where I stuck my middle finger out to the world, slept in, and went out for a walk in the splendid June afternoon. Calitain's weather during this season was fairly warm in the seventies.

The sun kindly kissed my skin, and I thought about stopping at a great coffee shop and grabbing my favorite cup of cappuccino. Yes, that's what today was supposed to be like, and the morning happened that way. I would have never guessed that afternoon would come, vanishing all my plans. On the other hand, a city like Calitain, diverse and electrifying in art and fashion culture, would be so fast-paced and trendy that it could win the coined word: big city. Given that, it wasn't unanticipated that time slipped away.

I ran my fingers through my hair with a sigh as I stared at the television displaying the news, sitting outside an electronics shop. It had happened again, but that wasn't the point. The most surprising thing was that they assigned the case to me. I guessed I should be proud. It was not a simple case to crack, but somehow it always found me. I must be great at my job for this kind of case to keep falling onto my lap. Being the best in the field, the thing I had to put up with was that I got assigned to tough cases, mostly homicides. I wasn't complaining. It was a joy to lock those bastards up. However, sometimes, it felt like it would be never-ending. If I locked one up, three more popped back in place. They were like weeds.

On the television, a woman. She looked familiar to a woman who visited me fifteen years ago, right before I moved to Calitain. The voice of a reporter:

"There is no news of the suspect in the case."

"Crazy, isn't it?" A guy next to me spoke, causing me to look away from the television. His height was around 5'7ft. Shorter than me in proximity. Too close to me for my comfort.

"For a country like Monthel, which got colonized just years ago by foreign entities and is trying to gain their independence," he shook his head, "such a despicable thing like murder?" He glanced at me and returned his gaze to the television. "What is this world turning into?"

I wasn't sure he directed the question to me, and if he expected us to share some kind of emphatic bond, then he was mistaken.

I stepped back, nodded my head out of politeness, and walked away. Still muddled with thoughts, I craved the coffee that got me out of my house. It was supposed to be my rest day. I tried my best to push the recent case out of my head—the crying woman on the television—out of my mind, but it was impossible, and by the time I walked into the cozy coffee shop, it was quite busy. I wasn't relaxed.

I've had many cases in my years as a cop. So many that I couldn't even count them, and it would be impossible for me to recall most of them. Some of them, though, did succeed to remain stuck in my brain like moles, bugging me at the wrong time. Some cases still surprised me and it reminded me that some people didn't deserve to be alive. Murderers.

I would never come to understand why some took the lives of others.

The thought was always perplexing to me. I had witnessed so many gruesome things in my life. It seemed like there was no limit to how imaginative murderers could be in the way they were killing their victims. I remembered my first time at a murder scene like it was yesterday. I had to run outside to puke my guts out. I didn't feel like myself the entire day after. Like my first murder case, the one from fifteen years ago was a case I will never forget. It was my last case before I had to move to Calitain.

I didn't bother going to the counter to order my coffee. I walked straight to a chair, took a seat, and rested my heavy head on the table. I tried to calm down. Maybe just the smell of coffee would help? It didn't help, and the crying woman's face made its way into my head again.

It reminded me of a woman who visited me fifteen years ago in Denton Falls.

JUNE 8TH, 2007, DENTON Falls

"Ma'am, you're not allowed in here like this," a junior officer, who acted like the precinct's receptionist, was shouting after a hysterically crying woman as they made their way into the office. Back then, I had yet to work my way up the ladder and shared an office with seven other cops in the same unit. I was in the process of clearing up my desk when the woman ran in, her face blotched up, tears running down everywhere, with her eyes wide and searching.

"Let go of me! I need to speak to someone!" the woman yelled, struggling with the junior officer that had held her forearm.

"What's going on here?" I asked, leaving everything, and walking towards them.

The woman's eyes flashed with recognition, and I recognized her, too. Only I never saw her this hysterical before. She ran out of the hold of the officer and ran towards me, clutching my hand tightly with hers.

"You. I remember you. You worked on the case, too, right? Do you remember me? My daughter? Her friend?" She rushed desperately at me.

I nodded. "Yes, Ma'am. Calm down, please." I looked at the junior officer and nodded at her to go, silently telling her that I would handle the situation. The woman was Gabriella's mother, one of the witnesses in the murder case we had just rounded up. She looked a little like her daughter. They had the same hair and olive skin. I'm guessing Gabriella got her eyes from her father, then. The woman in front of me looked like she used to be vibrant and beautiful, but the last weeks had taken a toll on her, and she was now looking ten years older. Her shoulder-length brunette hair was up in a messy bun, her pink lips chapped, and her pale skin looked red with all the tears. She had on a dress and a tote bag over her left shoulder and wore flip-flops on her feet. She must have been in a hurry to get here or was still struggling with everything and had yet to get her mind back long enough to care about her appearance.

"I need your help, please," she said, still holding my hands like she was scared I would disappear on her.

I nodded and edged backward a bit, pushing a seat with my leg to her and smiling with my eyes at her so she could relax. "I'm right here, Ma'am. I'm not going anywhere. Just take a breath and talk to me."

She sighed and reluctantly let go of my hand, taking a seat. I dragged a seat closer to her and sat facing her, too. There were only two guys inside the office with us, and they all had their attention on us both.

"I need you to help me find someone," she said in between muffled breaths.

She reached into her tote bag, brought out a book, and opened the book to show me the picture of a man. I took the photo out of the book to examine it more. The man didn't look familiar at all, so I looked up at her, curious for some clue or explanation. "My husband," she stated.

My eyes widened, and I returned to the picture, trying to look at it in a new light. "Gabriella's father?"

"Stepfather," she corrected, and I nodded because it made sense. He didn't have the eyes I remembered on Gabriella. "I need you to help me find him. He disappeared." She sobbed, covering her mouth with her palm. "He disappeared on the day of the incident. Never came back home."

"Why wasn't this brought up earlier?" I asked her about what I learned during the investigation. Her stepfather was out-of-town because of his truck-driving business, and the only representative for Gabriella, a minor, was her mum. "Do you think there was a motive for him to disappear?"

"He left home on March eighth and hasn't been back since. It's been three months since he left," she replied, with her hand running over her dampened hair.

I sighed. "I see. You should talk to someone else then." I glanced at my desk. I still had a lot to pack. "I'm about to be transferred." I added

"No, please." She grabbed my hands again. "Please help me find him. He has this truck business in Calitain. Something must have happened."

"Calitain?"

"Yes."

What were the odds? I shook my head. "That's where I'm being transferred to."

Her eyes gleamed with hope. "Oh, thank God, that's just perfect. Help me find him, please, help me out. I don't know what else to do."

I exchanged looks with my other colleagues, and they had no problem with it, so I promised her I would help.

I made a promise to that poor woman, and I could not keep it. It'd been fifteen years since I moved and came over to Calitain because my fiancé couldn't handle me being a cop, and there would be times when I would be unavailable. Sometimes, I would have to sleep out, either at the precinct or in a car. He didn't get that and got tired of waiting for me.

I was heartbroken when I applied for my transfer to a place 800 miles away from Denton Falls. I had seen a future with him. That good for nothing; I had thought he was the one. He swore he would never get tired and always be there for me. He made me go weak for the four-letter word called love. Because of him, I learned you should never rely on anything in the world unless it is concrete evidence backed by law and science. Gabriella's case was my last one. I had nothing left in that town for me, and I concluded it would be better if I had left. So, I shoved everything behind me and gave myself a clean slate. My fiancé leaving me wasn't the only thing that happened. I just needed a fresh start, and I believed Calitain would give that to me.

"Excuse me?"

A kind voice, that of a man, brought me back to the present, and I raised my head sharply off the coffee table, raising my brows at him. I frowned because I was just interrupted in my train of thought, and I didn't really like that. The young man cleared his throat. He looked to be a waiter. "Sorry, but what can I get you? You have to order."

"Oh, right." I relaxed my expression, sitting up straight. He meant no harm and was just doing his job. My mouth nearly opened up to say cappuccino, but then there was nothing calm or warm about my countenance and mood at the moment, and a cappuccino wouldn't stop me from thinking I was already on a roll. "I'll take an iced coffee."

That should do it.

"Just that?"

I nodded. "Yes, just that."

I watched him walk away, and my mind immediately returned to my train of thought. It was hard for me to call myself the best in the field because, for fifteen years, I had been unable to find one man. There was no way I was that inexperienced or Calitain was that vast. I knew it was a state in the country of Monthel. It had a population of 15 million according to its 2022 census data after the Covid virus hit its population. So, either the man was hiding, or he was just not on the surface of this planet anymore. Every angle I followed to find him led to a dead end. He was nowhere to be found. Maybe his daughter, Gabriella, had managed to find him. Maybe she knew where he was. I doubted she knew her mother had asked me to find him. If she did, she would have reached out to me, right? At least she would have been worried about her stepfather's whereabouts for fifteen years.

I thought about the case years ago, as I did now. Murders of innocent young girls. My mind went over everything I knew from back then and now, but I couldn't scratch off the itch in my back. Something was off, and something was fishy. This case was all too familiar to the one from fifteen years ago, which was strange because someone confessed to the crime back then and was still serving his time in jail. Could this be the work of a copycat?

CHAPTER FOUR

Brie

I should have told the police about the call. I felt like I should have let Clarissa know. Was it because the recent murders were familiar to fifteen years ago? Why did I suddenly feel like I had to share my story? No one knew about my past, and until now, I preferred it remained unknown.

Brie, focus on the meeting. Focus on the meeting. I kept repeating to myself. It was the only thing keeping me from plunging into hysteria. One thing I learned in dealing with my emotions was that if I could pick something to focus on, the rest would sort of fade into the background, and I could easily move along with my life.

After receiving that disturbing phone call, I spent a good number of minutes trying to calm myself down. My thoughts had been all over the place. As much as I tried to convince myself that it didn't happen and that it was all in my imagination, I knew the truth. It was real. Someone had called me and said the name I had never used in this place. Like in a trance, I locked my front door and got into my car. My boss had texted the address where I was to meet the witness, and I started to make my way there.

All the memories of Denton Falls that I kept hidden, threatened to overwhelm me, and it was only by sheer will that I kept myself from drowning in them. I moved to this town, Calitain, and I made a home for myself. I shoved my life in Denton Falls into a box and locked it. Now, the box was threatening to break open. Even now, as I rushed to meet the witness, a chill went through my body as I remembered that voice. Gabriella, he called me.

I glanced at my reflection in the tiny mirror in my bag. An eye shadow for my almond-shaped eyes will do the trick. I didn't want to appear tired, but presentable. One thing I loved about being a journalist was that it demanded a lot of time and commitment. That wouldn't sound right to anyone else but me. I loved to lose myself in my work. That way, I didn't have to think about my problems. It was fun, too, being a journalist. I got to experience an unending number of stories and meet interesting people while climbing the ladder of success.

My phone rang, and I jumped, antsy. I was wary as I picked it up with fear lodged in my throat. "Hello, this is Brie speaking," I said since the number wasn't one I had recognized.

"I-I was told to contact you." That had to be the witness, and I could tell by the way he stammered that he most likely had useful information for me.

"Are you at the meeting place?" I asked.

"Yes," he shakily replied.

"Sit tight. I'll be there in five."

We met at a local park, and I wasted no time getting there. If anything happened, if he were to leave, I wouldn't be able to question him anymore. It had happened before. There was a time when I got stuck in traffic on the way to meet with a witness to a crime. By the time I got there, the witness had disappeared. All efforts to find her proved abortive. Much later, we tracked her down, and she insisted that she had absolutely nothing to tell us. No matter how much we probed, she severely stood her ground. Our theory was that someone got to her before we did and convinced her to keep her mouth shut.

I walked into the park with just a minute to spare. It was great having a car. It sped things up. At this time in the morning, the park was empty. Except for the lone man sitting on the bench, no one else was there. I quickly made my way to him. He jerked up when he heard me approaching and cast nervous glances around.

"Good morning. My name is Brie Owen, it's nice to meet you." I stretched out my hand and he shook it.

"Dave."

If I had to guess, I would say that Dave couldn't be more than twenty years old. I've been with younger witnesses before. He had a buzz cut, making his features stand out. His eyes were blue, and he had a small scar beside his right eye. I noted all of this and tucked it somewhere in my head. I always did this with all the witnesses I met. No one knew when a description could save the day. He was wearing a blue hoodie and shorts. He looked scrawny.

I sat down beside him and began to record. I would still use my notes and pen, but my pen wouldn't be able to capture the tone of his voice when he answered my questions.

"Before we begin, I want to tell you that you don't have to be afraid of anything. There's nothing or no one that can hurt you here. I promise."

Dave took a deep breath. "Okay."

"Now," I flipped open my notepad, "can you tell me what you saw that day?"

"It was a man," he said, pressing his shaking hands together. "I should have done something. I should have tried to help her." He said as he rubbed his forehead.

"You don't have to feel guilty, Dave. Helping may go a long way. Trust me, I would know."

"Okay. It just all happened so fast," he muttered, folding in on himself. I didn't say anything, waiting for him to say more. "I was just walking in the woods when I thought I heard someone talking. I was going away, trying to give the person space. Maybe myself. I'm not good with people. So, I was going back the way I came when I heard this little girl scream." Dave shuddered, lost in memory. "I went back, just to see what happened; you know? All I saw was a girl on the ground. She wasn't moving. A man was standing above her, and I couldn't see his face. I was too scared to say anything, so I waited until he left." He spoke, nervously but sincerely, I sensed.

He looked so pained, and I could understand the guilt he must have been feeling. Witnesses were usually emotional. They either went through the incident but barely made it out or were helpless bystanders.

I was one on that day in the woods.

I barely made it out alive.

"Dave, did you get a good look at this man's profile?" I scribbled something down on my notepad.

"No... I only saw his back."

"What about the color of his clothes? What was he wearing?" I tapped the pen on the notebook. I needed more information.

"Man, I don't know." He closed his eyes, thinking. "I think it was a black shirt and maybe blue jeans. I'm not sure."

"What about his hair? Did you notice that?"

Dave let out a breath. "It was short. Stopped by his neck. I remember it was curly. I don't know what color it was."

I patted his knee. "Don't stress yourself, okay? It is better than having no information. If the police come to question you, tell them this exact information, too."

"The police?" he asked, fear resonating in his voice.

"Hey, you have nothing to be scared of," I said softly. "They'll only question you. You're not a suspect, okay?"

He nodded, still looking scared. I felt sorry for him. It was a classic case of being in the wrong place at the wrong time. Just like it happened to me. It was great for us, though, because now we had a lead on who the murderer could be. I felt my old fear rising as I thought about someone else who murdered a twelve-year-old. I had to get a grip on myself if I wanted to finish this up. I couldn't afford to be paralyzed by fear.

"Were you the one who called 191?" I asked him.

"Yeah. It seemed like the only thing I could do. I couldn't even go near the girl." He paused to take a breath. "But I saw it on the news and..." He shook his head.

I nodded grimly. He did the right thing by not contaminating the murder scene. The only thing anyone could hope for now was that the police would have enough clues and evidence to catch the killer.

I reached into my bag and brought out my business card. "Here," I said, handing it to Dave. "If you remember anything, anything at all, let me know. Call me anytime." Dave nodded.

"How did you get here?" I ran my eyes around, noticing only my car in the parking spots.

"My mum dropped me off." He stared at the business card.

"Come on," I said, pointing with my head at my car. "Where do you stay? I could just drop you off."

He stuffed his hands into the pockets of his hoodie. "No, I'm good. My mum is picking me up. Thanks, though... I guess."

Being I was a stranger, I understood he was hesitant about my offer. I wanted to reach out and hug him. I wanted to tell him that it wasn't his fault. He couldn't have known that some people just do evil, no matter what. But I waited at the park with him until his mother picked him up.

I walked to my unlocked car door and headed back home, mulling over the details I was able to get from him. My phone rang, and I glanced at it. It was Clarissa. I connected to my car's Bluetooth and picked up the call, thinking that phone calls would scare me for a long time.

"Are you done with the witness?" she asked.

"Yep. He's just a boy. Can't be more than twenty. He didn't get a good look at the murderer, but I got some information from him. Curly hair that stops at his neck and was wearing a black shirt over jeans."

"Oh, well, thousands of guys can fit that description in this town," she said, letting out a hopeless breath.

"That's why we should check footage from the surrounding buildings around the crime scene." I paused for a moment. "Do you think we could get access to those?" I asked.

"Maybe. Let me see if I can pull some strings," she replied.

"All right, as soon as you know something, let me know and I'll be on it."

My throat closed up as I remembered how the mother was wailing on the news. Something was tugging at my mind, telling me that this case was too similar to the one that happened fifteen years ago. I ignored the voice.

"Great. I'll have someone here get started on it. Draft me a story and send it to my email. I want it done in three hours. We have to be the first ones to put this story out."

"Copy that, boss."

At least I had something to focus on when I got home. Monsters, that was what people like that were. They snuffed out every bit of light and goodness they could find.

I GOT HOME AND HEADED straight to my kitchen with my stomach rumbling, letting my thoughts hang in the air. After making myself a meal, I opened my laptop and started working on the story, pulling details from my conversation with Dave. I didn't know if I was supposed to exclude his name, so I underlined it with a footnote for Clarissa to see. On my notepad, I dated the news story—June 2022, making sure the dates weren't mixed up. It wasn't a technique or a necessity for a journalist. It was just me, a lone wolf who covered many crime stories in a day.

Didn't want to mix up the dates. I read through it once and fixed the mistakes before sending the file.

I thought then would be a good time to catch up on Friends, my favourite show. I made myself comfortable in front of the TV and heard my phone ringing just as the episode started. I sighed and got up, wondering what Clarissa could want from me now. Perhaps she wanted me to fix something in the article I sent her. I thought about it for a second—would she really be calling at such late hours? Just as I caught myself in that thought, I realized it wasn't Clarissa calling me. Although my mind screamed not to pick up, I was still answering the call, anyway.

"Hello, this is Brie speaking." Fear took over my throat as I sent a prayer to whoever was listening that it should be anyone else.

A low chuckle came from the other side.

"Hello, Gabriella. What do you wish for?"

My mind went numb. I couldn't ignore it now.

"My, my. How much you have grown."

I was still standing, petrified to my bones. I had the good sense to force myself to end the call, not interested in whatever the voice would say next.

"How?" I whispered brokenly to myself. "How is this happening?" I felt a single tear shed.

The voice was petrifying and familiar; a shrilling whisper that made my bones shake. I gritted my teeth at the sound, and my soft skin was marked with a bruise from the worms crawling on them. I trembled as I did fifteen years ago. Behind my walls, I heard a whisper lurk. I could almost swear that he was right behind me or that his looming shadow was hanging above me.

There was a buzzing sound before someone was at my door. My door alarm buzzed, and it was still ringing.

A hard knock and a silhouette of a man were next to my window. I shuddered as I took a fetal position. I hid underneath my covers, but I couldn't seem to understand what I was afraid of. Was it the man outside of my door or the shadows lurking in my dream? The piercing thoughts told me to tell the truth about what happened that day in the woods.

CHAPTER FIVE

Detective Anita

I stared out my office windows down at the busy streets. Being a detective for over seventeen years had its perks, and one of them was getting my own comfortable and private office on the top floor of the precinct. From up here, I could see a whole lot of the city. I could see people running around and living their normal lives, chasing after one thing or another. It was our job to keep them safe from criminals, it was my job to catch the evil among them and put them behind bars, and so far, all these years, I'd been doing great at it.

Walking up the ladder in this world of law enforcement wasn't an easy feat, and it had required years of demanding work and sleepless nights. Right from when I was little, I had always wanted to be a cop. My dad worked as a night guard for a security company, he always told me gruesome stories whenever he came back to talk about his day, considering that my mum was never really interested in them.

For a seven-year-old girl, these stories should have given me nightmares, but they gave me the zeal to grow up one day to be able to fight injustice. Every time I listened to them, their endings would give me a sense of peace when my dad would say: "And another bastard was locked up."

He used the word bastard a lot, though mum hated it and even warned him to not say it anymore because I was a young girl. For me, the fact that justice prevailed, in the end, made me grow up wanting to fight the bad guys. In dad's stories, the ending was always a win from good versus evil, but in reality, I had come to learn that sometimes it was evil that won. I never really wanted to, but I couldn't help doubting dad's stories, were they real or made up? After all, he had a dream of being a writer one day.

I wanted to fight the bad guys and protect the innocents. I had no regrets, though not all my cases had been successful. I had caught some and lost some, but the good outweighed the bad, and a particular case was a pain in the neck.

There was no way it was this familiar and not suspicious, was it? How can the same crime happen with so many years of difference between them and when the culprit of the first crime was still in jail? I had checked multiple times and there was no record of him breaking out. He confessed to the crime, even if evidence stated otherwise. At that time, I wasn't the lead detective, so I couldn't overturn the confession as evidence.

A knock on the door startled me, and I turned away from the windows to see Darwin standing beside my open door, one hand on it and another holding a file. Darwin was my colleague, and we'd cracked a couple of cases together. He was good at his job despite being at the rank he was.

"Good day, Detective Anita," he greeted with a small, courteous smile.

I sighed and gestured at him to come in. We'd worked together for years, yet he still called me that. I couldn't get him to stop. I concluded that he was just very professional and, therefore, preferred to address me that way. "Good day, Darwin." I relaxed my body on my table and rubbed my temples. I could already feel a headache coming. My table was scattered with files of the recent case I was on, and it was bugging me.

Darwin's eyes flicked over my table and back to me. "Tough one, isn't it?"

I groaned. "Yes, one of those pains. It's just crazy and feels like déjà vu." I couldn't fight off the fact that this seemed familiar to the case from fifteen years ago. They had too many similarities. I wasn't supposed to disclose my case to anyone, but Darwin was a fellow detective, and since moving to Calitain, we had worked together and had an excellent work relationship. We made a good team most of the time.

I remembered the woman I saw on the television and the woman in the precinct back in Denton Falls years ago. No mother should have to go through that. Those girls had experienced horrible things that shouldn't be happening. It couldn't go on. I felt like I was the one responsible to put an end to it.

"Déjà vu?" Darwin asked, frowning. "Does it have the same pattern?"

"The MO, yes." I pulled my swirl chair back and took a seat. "But it shouldn't be, and I don't understand how it's possible. A similar case happened years ago, and it was closed."

"The criminal was caught?"

"Yes, and is still serving time as we speak. He confessed to the crime, so I don't know what's happening." I rubbed my forehead. "Why would a similar case come up now?" I said as I looked out the window as if a response were to come flying to me. "It's just...odd. Why after all these years?"

Darwin exhaled loudly and sat in one of the chairs opposite to me, facing my table and looking over the papers and pictures. "Two heads are presumed to be better than one, so lay it on me. my case is on trial, and I could help you with this without intruding. Just think out loud."

I gave him a grateful look. "The only thing I know for sure now is that the girl is still out there. Gabriella should be living her life normally now and free of worries. She was only twelve years old when it happened, and she should have moved on. I don't know where she is, and up until this case, I didn't think I needed to know, though I worried about her sometimes."

"She was the only witness," stated Darwin.

"No, not at all." I tugged a bit at my ponytail. I liked my hair packed tightly up and away from my face whenever I was busy and thinking.

"There were three." Memories from that gory day flooded my mind, and there was a reason why that case had yet to leave my head after fifteen years. "Sean, who was heavily under the influence of drugs, and Eve... I still worry about her sometimes. I don't think she ever recovered." I tapped my fingers on the side of my head. "Something keeps bugging me that the real culprit isn't the one in prison."

"Why do you say so? It's been fifteen years. Similar crimes happen from time to time," Darwin said, crossing his arms over his chest.

"No, no." I leaned closer to the table, my hands grabbing papers and pictures. "This is way too similar, Darwin. The girls..." I pointed at a picture, turning it in his direction. "Look, the girls are poised the same way." It was a picture from fifteen years ago. I pushed another picture from the recent case to him, comparing them side by side. "Their facial expressions." My heart was racing now, and I knew I wasn't just seeing things. "The familiarity, do you see it?"

"I do," Darwin said, brows furrowed as he stared at the two pictures. "There's something about them."

"Yes." I wasn't sure whether to be happy that I wasn't going crazy after all and there were similarities or be sad because what happened fifteen years ago wasn't something that should be happening again. I would have preferred if I was losing my mind and seeing things that were not there. "It could be a copycat" I muttered to myself, chewing on my bottom lip.

Did I need to look in harder, or was this all there was to the case? What had I not seen? What could I have missed? Was I not doing my job like I should? Was I failing all these victims and their families?

"It could be," Darwin agreed. "Criminals tend to copy each other as some kind of delirious loyalty or just because they want to seem as important."

"There's something else you need to know," I said, leaning onto the table again. "Fifteen years ago, the children had different testimonies. The judge ruled out the inconsistencies, but now I think something could be there. Sean said there were seven people, Eve said there were five, and Gabriella said four."

Darwin stared at me. "Who could have been lying? And why?"

"I do not know, but there has to be something fishy, right?" I asked him pensively. "No one can blame Eve because she got admitted to a psych ward, that poor girl. So, if we were to find something, it should be between Sean—"

"And Gabriella," Darwin interrupted, nodding as a sign that he understood.

The office got silent as I thought about the children. Sean and Gabriella... Sean was in jail, and Gabriella was just twelve years old at that time. What could she possibly have known? Was there anything there, or was I just barking up the wrong tree?

"Wait," Darwin broke the silence, and I broke off my train of thought to stare at him. "Does this case have anything to do with the man you asked me to find?" He raised the file he had brought in with him earlier. "Because I got a pretty solid lead."

"What?" I sat up straight, repeating what he had just said in my mind.

"I finally got a lead on the man you asked me to find. It wasn't easy, but I think this is not a dead end again. I even got some pictures and addresses." He confidently said as he placed the file in my hand.

I took the file from Darwin, my heart beating loudly as I opened it up, getting the content out, and the picture I gave him was at the top. It was the picture that Gabriella's crying mother had given to me fifteen years ago that had proved useless until now. My eyes lit up with hope. "You're sure it's not a dead end?"

Darwin shrugged. "It doesn't seem so now. You know we can't tell until all is done. It's just a solid lead for now."

I sighed, understanding him. "Yeah, sorry." My eyes skimmed through the information on the papers, and I couldn't help the small smile that wanted to fight its way to the surface. "This is more information than I've found in the last years trying to find this man. Excellent job, Darwin."

"No problem." He smiled. "Is it related to the murder case?"

I spread the information apart. One of the details was an address to what I presumed was where Gabriella's supposed stepfather was. The other utility bills with his name, Daniel Caravan.

"Of course, there was no way he could have just fallen off the earth," I said.

He disappeared on March eighth. The same day the incident happened. Rumour had it that he ran away, but something didn't sit right, and I was supposed to have found him years ago. I always thought he knew how to blend in, either that, or I'd been doing a shitty job all this while. The dates on utility bills dated thirteen years from the day he disappeared.

Something would keep catching my eye. He stopped paying his bills some years ago; had we caught a trail of him years after he had disappeared again? Was he still at the address on the bill? Or was someone using his name? That could be possible. Identity theft wasn't new, especially for people from a remote place like Denton Falls who had no credit history of being traced and one whose family hadn't filed his death certificate, because hopes were still held on him being alive. Gabriella's mum had that hope on the day she came to see me at the precinct.

"Something must have happened to him, right?"

Darwin shrugged. Of course, he had no answer to that. It was a sort of rhetorical question. "Trust you to remember even the tiniest detail from a case fifteen years ago."

"This is one special case, Darwin, very special."

"So, it is related," he said inquisitively.

I shrugged. "I don't know. I honestly cannot say at the moment. Anything could have happened to this man. He could have just run like the rumours said, not man enough to end his marriage well, or it could be something else. I'm leaning more towards the second option, to be honest, something feels off about this man."

"How crazy is it that you got assigned to the same kind of case?"

I pressed my thumb against my temple, still trying to connect the dots. "I must have something unresolved then." I thought I was an extreme kind of workaholic until I met Darwin. With his rugged look that sometimes made people think he was a criminal before he became a cop, he was a very hard-working man, and we would stay up late at the precinct even after everyone was gone, solving cases, and trying to think of solutions. The dead of the night always brought some kind of peace and quietness that the brain needed to dot I's and cross T's.

Fifteen years ago, I was still a rookie and just wanted to solve as many cases as possible and save people. Now, after working as a detective for all these years, I was sure something was off about this case and the one from a year ago when the recent killing began. I couldn't just leave it alone. I had to dig in deeper and satisfy my curiosity. What stone had I left unturned? What did I need to revisit? All I had from the case fifteen years ago were the witnesses, and so far, the location of two was known and accounted for.

Two. Except for Gabriella.

I pushed myself and my chair until I was facing my computer, and I quickly turned it on, grateful for the fact that, as a detective, I had access to the records of everyone in the database. I typed in Gabriella's full name and watched in satisfaction as the computer brought up her details.

"Journalist," I read as I leaned back on my chair, fingers finding my chin.

"What?" Darwin asked; I had almost forgotten that he was here.

"Gabriella is a journalist now." I nodded at the screen. "Something is off here, and I will get to the bottom of it. I swear."

Nothing would stop me this time.

CHAPTER SIX

Brie

I'm back to that other nightmare. Eve covers her mouth with her hand. She giggles and then crawls into a tent, one her mum had built for us that evening after Eve had pleaded with her in a sing-song voice: "Mum, let's go camping, sit around a fireplace and watch the stars." A request she knew her mum would frown upon. For the eight years I had known Eve, she was only allowed to go to two places. School and her room.

Mrs. Willie, in my opinion, either saw Eve as an egg that could be easily cracked, even broken without her parents there, or she might have had psychic powers that foretold her that Eve would someday not be the same girl she gave birth to, so she shielded her from the world. Whichever option it was, they both seemed rather disturbing to me.

Her excitement ignited that evening when I was there for the sleepover. I shuffled a deck of cards I had bought at the flea market with my pocket money. The image of that evening replayed in my mind. Especially when Mrs. Willie opened the door to Eve's room, and we both ducked under our covers in the tent, the deck of cards hidden under my pillow as we faked snoring. Eve's mum took a peek into the tent and then walked out. I turned towards Eve, and she had fallen fast asleep.

Then, the worms are back. The part of the nightmare that floods me with fear. I'm locked inside a box. Darkness overwhelms me. Above me, a shuffling sound, like I'm being buried under the earth. I scream, my hand banging against the wooden box. Something crawls over my skin. It begins its way up my toes, and I try to shake my foot, but it's bound with something. The crawlers make their way toward my hands. I jerk it, but it slams against something wooden.

With a hard knock, my knuckles smack against a wooden box. How long have I been in the box? Did someone put me in here? I open my mouth to scream, but I gurgle. In my throat and mouth, a slimy taste. I gag. I try to vomit whatever is in my mouth, but there is a polythene bag over my head. Taking tiny breaths at the moment is the hardest thing I have ever done. A cracking sound around my ribs area. Pain lodges right through me.

"Help."

I lose the word in the gurgle. Then comes a shuffling sound, like one is digging into the earth. A cackle echoes like firecrackers. It resonates within the cold ground against my skin.

I reach my hand around the wooden box, but my hand rubs over something cold. I pat over it, dewy. It's a face of a human, perhaps. I gag again. The face of the girl in the hut plays into my imagination. Her pale skin is like the statue of the weeping lady with a veil. One I had read once was called The Weeping Virgin. A vengeful soul who lost her husband on the night of their marriage to a group of bandits and was back from the abyss to take their souls with her into purgatory. With her weeping eyes and what was called black tears, the girl in the hut looked similar to her: vengeful.

I freeze. On my skin are crawling worms. They cover my hand with a puddle. I try to clean my face with my hand, but the worms are coming from my hands. "Help," I say, more out of breath this time.

Drenched in sweat, I woke up to my alarm clock. The sun was out, and I could feel its burning rays on my skin. The worms are back, the one thing that threatened my existence. It gagged the life out of me. Or were they the lies I had told so far? If I were, to tell the truth, would the worms be gone forever? The skin around my neck felt wet as I ran my hand towards it, the slimy feel of the worms still alive to my senses.

That nightmare hadn't reoccurred in a while until the voice of the one who brought about my nightmares called me the previous night.

I walked towards the door to ensure that the shadow of last night was gone. There was an envelope taped to my door. It read, "To Gabriella." I deliberated between opening it or pretending to not see it and throwing it out. A foreboding enigma lay behind the red envelope. I unsnapped its edge. There was another envelope with the words: "Hello, Gabriella. What do you wish for?"

I opened the second envelope. My eyelids raised a bit as I looked at it. Just numbers? A phone number? I brought out my phone and dialed Clarissa's number.

"Hey, I need to speak to you about something. It's urgent."

I would rather face this game than run away. So, whatever your name is or whatever smirk you have on your face at the moment, I can't wait to take that off. I walked briskly into the company, looking like a train that would not be derailed. A sense of urgency took over the air as writers, columnists, and even editors looked to clear their tables as quickly as possible.

"Hello, Brie!" yelled the marketing assistant who was making his way out of the marketing department. He is always cheerful, I thought.

"Hello, Mark," I replied, not pausing for a moment. I was a woman on a mission, and everything else outside my thoughts seemed non-existent.

The office oozed with numerous activities as some reporters and photographers left toward the streets to gather new stories. One could see different sectors fanning the crime taking the lead while sports and civic issues followed closely behind. These guys were the real superheroes when it came to gathering top-quality information ready to be consumed. It was a tough and delicate job. I was glad I worked there.

When the data, stories, and photos, had been collected throughout the day, filing the reports began. At this time, the editing desk would start to function. They would be editing the filed stories and photo captions and giving them good headlines and sub-heads. After a list of stories had been compiled from not only the company staff reporters but news agencies as well, a decision on which stories to print would then be made. Not only for which page but also for which part of the page. The page-making process would come right after, with the most impor tant stories at the top, while lighter stories would go to the bottom as anchors.

I headed for Clarissa's office. I could have gone to the associate editor, but after a news report, I made two months into working with Eagle's daily, which was a choice of newsworthy and a most-told story, a clash of opinions led to me confiding in my chief editor rather than the assistant editor. Adam hated my guts. To him, I wasn't following protocol to get ranked in the company. Clarissa got me, and I worked better with her than Adam.

I pushed open a glass door with metal knobs, on which was calligraphy with the words: Clarissa Adam, Chief Editor. I was going to recount my ordeal on the phone to my boss, about the devastating past. At first, I had so many questions: How did he get my number? Why did he wait for fifteen years? Why was it me, back then and now?

I thought the law would have caught up to him or nature would have taken him, but he was my age-long nightmare and had returned to haunt me again. This and many more questions without answers raced through my mind. It had been fifteen years since my unfortunate encounter with the mystery man, and the memories flooded in like they had happened yesterday. His words played in my head in a timeless loop.

"Hello, Gabriella. What do you wish for?"

That wish of his, one that played fate towards me being alive. I brought my hand to my ears, the timeless loop still playing.

Silence, I screamed to my inner mind as a replay of his known, yet unfamiliar face appeared.

My body was still shaking from the chill I felt while I answered the phone and realized it was the same monster who greeted me with that terrible glare almost fifteen years ago in the hut where I was supposed to meet Sean. How could I be haunted all these years by one single unfortunate memory, yet it was almost becoming my reality again?

I could barely survive a day without the thought creeping into my mind. Still, one thing had changed. I was now in a position to fight, and there would be no stopping me now.

"Good morning!" Clarissa said.

I didn't even realize I hadn't knocked before barging into her office. The urgency and train of thought made me gasp for air.

"Take a seat, Brie. It sounds like you have a lead?"

I took a seat and began to narrate the ordeal to her. "What?" Her eyes widened in surprise, and she looked at me in a state of mild shock. But before I could go on and recount the event from earlier, a call came in for her, so she took a moment to attend to it. At that moment, the flashbacks returned.

I could see her. I could see Eve, my best friend, vividly in a trance...

I smiled as I was taken back through the times when everything was fine. I could see Eve and I playing and running the night before the incident.

March 8th, 2007, Denton Falls

Eve's face lit with so much joy and excitement. I was the happiest about getting the opportunity to spend a girl's night together again. I was thriving, trying my hands on some of the things I had always wanted to do. I had so much fun.

I was there because it allowed me to sneak off to see my crush, Sean. Not like I wasn't there for Eve, but the thought of seeing him again took precedence over other things. We had devised a perfect plan to meet in our usual spot, and that was all I could think of all night long. But who gave me the confidence to go through the woods alone at that time? I thought to myself.

"It was worth it, I guess." I continued to ponder.

It was not the first time Sean and I would be meeting secretly in the woods. It had been going on for a little while now. That was our only way of seeing each other since my mum didn't approve of our friendship. I could also remember how Eve chased me down the woods the morning after our girl time together. She was just the clingiest girl ever. How did she even wake up and sneak behind me into the woods? I thought. I didn't make any unnecessary sound that could have woken her up. Did I?

Eve was also very stubborn. I could not send her back home. She definitely wouldn't have listened. She was also interested in finding out why and where her friend was off to at that time of the morning. Despite being tired, Eve didn't give up her quest either. She was so curious as I would not tell her where I was heading, and I also needed a companion through the woods. A companion I would no longer need when Sean crossed my eyesight.

Sean was the ideal boy, at least for me. Our paths crossed at the park very close to my house, and ever since our first encounter, my crush on him blossomed. He was out riding his bicycle at the park when we met and he offered me a ride around the park on his bicycle, which I wasn't going to decline.

We had so much fun together riding on Sean's bike all evening long when both of us decided to meet again soon. I would often visit the park just to get the opportunity to see and hang out with my crush. I never missed the chance to do so. We got ice cream and burgers sometimes, too, and would sit together at the park to eat them. We were the dream young movie couple.

Our friendship was growing rapidly, and Sean would oftentimes ride me home on his bicycle.

We seemed like we were made for each other.

Sean equally liked me as much as I liked him.

He was always looking forward to a meeting whenever we could.

My mum had taken notice of my new friend and didn't approve of our relationship. She asked me to steer clear of the boy because he influenced me badly. He hung around the wrong people and had no roots, which was the word she referred to for someone who was an orphan. But she didn't get what she wanted; her warning only made me want to see him more often.

Sean also knew my mum had scolded me many times for hanging out with him, and that was how we came up with the plan to meet in the hut in the woods whenever an opportunity presented itself. By opportunity presenting itself, I mean we had to make it happen ourselves because, without a valid reason, my parents would not let me out of the house. For a moment, I swore I got a glimpse of Eve's life.

The sleepover seemed like the perfect excuse, and it worked. Eve and I had fun after our homework, playing numerous games before eventually going to bed. I had snuck out of the house in the early morning hours and made for the woods to meet Sean. I ensured not to wake anyone, and after running for a bit, I was in his arms.

However, our meeting was short-lived. I could not stay any longer than we both would have hoped. My parents did not approve of the meeting, so we were merely risking a lot to make it happen. To be able to see each other again secretly, I had to leave as quickly as possible. I promised we could do it again soon, but I had to hurry back to the house before anyone noticed I was missing. I gave Sean a long, tight hug before returning to Eve's room. He and I met a couple more times after that, and it didn't seem like anything would go wrong, until it became an eternal nightmare for me.

"So, you think whoever contacted you is the same man from your past?" Clarissa asked, her eyes staring at me as I narrated the incident. But it couldn't be him, I thought, it couldn't.

I watched her flick on her pen. For the past years that I had worked with Clarissa, I had noticed that this gesture meant she was interested in what you had to say. This gesture was always followed by, "So, how is this connected to the story you are following at the moment?"

She stared at the glassy wall of her grey-painted office adorned with a large portrait of her achievements and photos from her years as a photojournalist.

I continued the recount of my past event, the MO of the dead girls on the TV with the rue flower, then concluded, "I think we can help the police solve this case and bring justice to the family of the bereaved."

"Sure, let's run with it."

I could feel pain in my temple, and I pressed my fingers into it.

"What is it, Brie?" she asked.

"The killer left me to find a package."

"What was in the package?" she asked, her voice down to a whisper.

"Just this. I think it's a phone number, but I don't know." I handed over the envelope to her, and she examined it carefully.

"This doesn't look like a phone number. God, this is huge. For once, we're not writing the story. We get to be the story!"

I wished I could share half of her excitement, but I focused on keeping myself sane and alive.

"You know what? I know just the guy. He can find anything, and I'm sure he'll get to the bottom of what these numbers mean. I'll give him a call now."

I watched as my editor dialed a number and wrote down an address. "Update me every step of the way," she said before sending me off.

The address she gave to me was that of a shop.

IT LOOKED LIKE A JUNK shop with all the broken devices at the entrance. It was open, so I just strode in, looking behind me to ensure I wasn't being followed. I couldn't get rid of the feeling that someone was watching me.

"Hello. How may I help you?" A clean-shaven man in a white T-shirt looked up at me. On the table, it seemed he was typing into a tablet. Connected to it were cords, and it made a whirring sound.

"Uh, I was sent here by—" I began.

He brought his hand to the side of his face, tapping on his ears. I noticed he had wireless earphones on.

"Oh! You're the reporter Clarissa sent!" He snapped his finger. "Come on, follow me!"

I followed him down a dimly painted stairwell, which seemed worn out from the overstepped feet, into a backroom that seemed like a dungeon. It was dark with multiple monitors whose light brightened the room. On each screen, different encrypted data was jargon to me.

"Do you, have it?" His words snapped me to concentration. I flipped open my notebook, where the numbers I copied from what was in the envelope were on one of its pages. There was no way I would just hand the whole envelope to him. I watched him unfold the paper. "Is this like a conspiracy thing? Or are you investigating a criminal?"

"A little of both, actually," I muttered.

"Hmm, this doesn't look like a phone number." He frowned. "The looks more like coordinates to me." He sat in front of one of his large screens and typed something too fast for me to follow. "Yep, I was right. Looks like you're going on a road trip."

I stared at the location on the screen, fear uncurling in my gut. This wasn't good, but I had to stop somewhere first, my nemesis. I had three of them, and I was paying a visit to one of them now.

CHAPTER SEVEN

The Genie

I watched as her eyes fluttered open. I waited in silence as she came to her senses and realized what was going on. She jerked up suddenly and stared at me. Introductions were in order. "I'm a genie, and I make people's wishes come true. Like you, she was in a desperate moment of her life when I became her genie." I cackled. "Now, she makes my dreams come true. Don't look at me that way," I said as I tilted my head slightly. "That was the same look my mum gave me when I was nine. Guess what I did?" I asked with a smile. "I snapped the neck of her lovely bird."

I smiled gleefully at the look of horror on her face. I thought she was beautiful. She had dark hair that shone and large doe eyes. She should be glad that I was doing this for her. It was what she wanted anyway.

Her name was Mary. And just in case she would change her mind, I made sure her hands and legs were tied firmly to a chair bolted to the floor.

I kneeled in front of her, drying the tears that rolled down her cheeks. "It wasn't my fault. The thing is, that damn bird was so annoying. It was always yipping every morning." I shook my head in distaste, remembering the awful sound the bird was always making. I hated it so much. "It was like it knew the wrong time to open that cursed beak. It would make noise whenever I stared out the window at my neighbors. I just couldn't take it anymore, you know?" I said as I felt my skin burn.

I didn't expect any answer, and I knew I wouldn't get one. I took a deep breath and walked to the window. It was sunny outside. I hated sunny days. They looked like they were forcing everyone to be bright and cheerful when they felt the opposite. That was why I hated mornings. They were dreadful. My mother told me to make haste while the sun was shining. I called it bullshit.

I started speaking softly, almost as if to myself, but I knew she could hear me.

“My mum, you could call her the praying type. There was nothing like me having girls as friends. I had no access to a computer. No cellphone. Just the Bible. And that bird was always sitting there, snitching on me when I took glances at the neighbor’s daughter. My mum said, ‘You are the son of the devil.’ The very next day, she locked me up in an asylum.”

I smiled at the memory of the bird lying dead in my palms. The eyes had been open, except there was no longer life in them this time. It was thrilling. It was a beautiful moment. I believe that some things that happen to us have a major hand in shaping us to be who we are. The moment I killed that bird was a defining moment for me. I felt like I was truly seeing myself. Knowing myself. My mother hadn’t thought so, though. In fact, she had the very opposite thinking.

I grew up with no technology, looking confused as my classmates talked about cartoons and video games. Didn’t their mothers raise them like mine was raising me? I used to ask myself. My mother’s voice whispered in my ear. “He whom the father loves, he chastises.”

I raked my fingers through my hair. “My doctor, Mr. Grey, a frail-looking old man... He said I had an antisocial tendency or disorder or some other gibberish. I wasn’t listening. My mother burst into tears when he told her. I didn’t know why she was crying. Now I know. She was regretting giving birth to me. Oh, and be sure, I would make her regret it.”

I knew Mary didn’t understand, but it didn’t matter. She didn’t need to understand to listen. I walked to her and squatted down, so we were nearly eye to eye. “Imagine my surprise when I... I knew what I could do. I could see right through people. Through their pretenses and hypocrisies. I could make their darkest wishes come true." Her muffled scream from under the tape caught my attention, and I stared for a moment at the tape covering her mouth.

"You need to stop that and let me finish the story. You need to listen to me." I paused and ran my palms over my face. "One of my teachers told me that I could make people do things, which is why I could make her do what she did. I granted her wish, and now she lives her life as I wish." I smiled at the thought but could hear Mary desperately gasping for air. "Hush now." I patted her head gently like a mother would pat a child she loved. "I know how much you have detested the air you breathe. I'm going to grant your wish tonight." My face broke out in a grin.

I had been watching her for a while now. For about two weeks, I followed her home from work, trailing behind so she wouldn't notice me. I was there when she sat on a bench and cried her eyes out. I hid in the trees, and she thought she was alone. That was why she felt safe enough to bawl. People always showed who they were when they thought no one was watching. They shed all the pretense and hypocrisy and showed their true-self. She worked as a nurse and always complained to her fellow workers that the job was too stressful. I knew about all of this. I saw through her. I saw all her hopes, dreams, and struggles.

I was there when she got drunk and screamed that she wanted to die.

I was there when she yelled that she wanted someone to kill her because she had no guts to do it herself.

I was there at the bar with her, watching over her, like an angel.

She didn't once glance at me, and it made my job easier. Sometimes, they recognized me, and I had to do extra work to fulfill their wishes. It was only on a few occasions that I had to move on to someone else.

Unlike what my mother thought, I was very smart. I knew how to protect myself. I protected myself from her well enough.

Mary didn't notice when I followed her home again. The only difference was that she wasn't going to sleep in her house this time. She was going with me. I made sure she got to her house. When she was about to reach her doorway, I covered her mouth from behind with a handkerchief I had doused with anesthesia. Her body went limp in my hand, she looked perfect, and I used the cover of darkness to place her in the large bag I had brought.

I waited until she got home, knowing she lived in a secluded area, and no one would see me. No one would ever know what happened to her. Unlike superheroes, I wasn't interested in taking credit for those I had saved. My generosity went way further than wanting recognition, it meant more to me.

With care, I removed the duct tape I used to shut her up when she let out an ear-piercing scream. I winced. One thing I learned was that people were usually too scared to take action themselves. That was why I had taken it upon myself to grant them their deepest, darkest desires. It was also why I had a soundproof room.

That was what I did for Hailey when she wanted her mother gone. Though she cried a lot when her mother was gone, I knew she would finally be free. Or what I did for Carrie when she said she hoped her boyfriend died. Or Grace, I did what she asked for: oh, if she died, she would be much better, no one would even miss her. They would all look back and realize that I did them a favour.

"Please—" Mary choked out. "I beg you..."

"Shhh." I placed a finger on her lips. "It will all be over soon," I said and caressed her hair. A courtesy my mum wouldn't have extended to me.

I stood up and walked to the opposite side of the room. I picked something up and turned back to her. Her eyes were brown. How did I not see that before? Oh, that's right. I always watched her from behind. The colour of her eyes was the same shade of dress my mother wore when—I shook my head. There was no need for all those useless sentiments. I needed to be clear-headed.

She started crying. She pleaded for me to spare her life, and I couldn't help smiling at her act. I saw right through her. I knew that inside she was grateful her wish would be granted.

"You don't understand... Please. I'll do anything."

I frowned at her. She struggled with the bindings, and I knew she could never get out of it.

"I'm only granting your wish. I told you I'm a genie. I'm granting you your wish to die by another's hands."

"No! I didn't mean it!" She sobbed.

I walked towards her; every step measured. She was still screaming, trying to kick out her legs. I reached for her and looked down at her.

"Mary, it will all be over soon," I whispered in her ear.

Then there was silence. Blissful silence.

CHAPTER EIGHT

Detective Anita

I reached into my fridge for a can of beer. Fifteen years ago, I made a promise to Gabriella's mother. I wondered what she looked like now. Had she moved on, or was she holding to a thread of hope that he would come back home someday?

Her daughter was a journalist and might have found him sooner than I did. I will try to find her later. According to her profile, she now went by the name Brie Owen. She was a crime reporter for Eagle's daily newspaper. After such a gruesome incident, I thought she would live a different life, one that was away from the crime scene. I couldn't help but think she always hid something, there was a piece of truth she wished to keep untold, I was sure.

A surge of urgency brushed through me. I snapped the beer can open and stared at my wall. The address from the investigation file for Daniel and the utility bills, of course. In a modern-day like this, in a big city like Calitain, it was hard for one to be untraceable, especially when they had utility bills. It didn't make sense. I couldn't seem to understand why it had taken me fifteen years to find him.

I stared at the picture of the brown-eyed, wavy-haired Veronica Clooney, a twelve-year-old victim from Denton Falls, fifteen years ago. Before she died, her foster mum had reported her missing. For such a small town with a population of 9,467, according to its census data in 2015, no one took her missing case seriously because she was a troubled girl. She hung out with the wrong crowd, always ran away from her foster parent's home, and came back after days, weeks, or even months. No one took the case seriously until the phone line rang that early morning of March eight and there was a report of a dead girl in a secluded hut in the woods.

She was different from the recent victims. Their facial symmetry, economic backgrounds, geographical area, and age varied. The only thing that tied both cases together was the fetus' poise and the rue flower, which was found beside Veronica when we arrived, and a young boy at that time confessed to killing her. The investigation reports on my wall still gave me chills, no matter how many times I had seen them. These clues were like a jigsaw puzzle until I put them together to make meaning.

"Wait a minute," I said like I was speaking to another person in the room. My detective instinct kicked in. The curious cat wasn't ready to sleep, I wanted to solve something, find meaning in something. The date of the last utility bill was on February 12, 2020. I traced the line from the bill to the date of the first victim in the recent killing. Thirteen years later, after Sean was arrested. My eyes widened and focused, it's the same date, I thought. It couldn

't be a coincidence.

My phone buzzed. A text message, its sender unknown. "Brie will be at 9929 Creek Ridge Street. Rivers, Calitain 1622, tomorrow afternoon." Brie? What had it got to do with the case? Creek Ridge? Where have I seen that name? I ran my eyes on the utility bill again.

Daniel Caravan.

Electric bill due of $74.

Address: 9929 Creek Ridge Street. Rivers, Calitain 1622.

The puzzle seemed to be assembling itself. Seemed too convenient to be true. I decided to do what I did best: my job. I would stake out until she arrived at the location.

CHAPTER NINE

Brie

Even though they had made sure I had no metal object on me, I held my breath while going through the metal detector, afraid of whom I would meet or what I would discover or realize on my visit to the prison. After providing all my details, I told the officer whom I wanted to see. Then he took me to the visiting area, where physical contact was allowed. Sean had been behaving well.

My eyes wandered as I waited, and as much as I tried, I couldn't help observing a family who came to see their incarcerated mother. My mind began to think of things she might have done, but it must have been the foul stench wafting into my nostrils that caused me to trail off. The prison's smell was between body odour, stale air, cleaning supplies, and for some reason, spicy foods. It wasn't my first visit, but the smell differed every time. My hands begged to be placed somewhere as they sat on my lap. I was scared to put my hands on the steel top of the table. As usual, I shuddered as my skin touched the cold metal.

I saw him walk into the room, escorted by a guard, and thought if the cuffs around his wrist were also cold. I smiled weakly as he sat. He returned my smile, and tears trickled down my cheek. It was more due to the memories than the sight of him.

"Now, Brie, no need for that." His voice had gotten huskier, I noted as I wiped my cheek. I tried to speak, but my voice failed me. All I wanted was to tell him how much I longed to hug him and needed him to tell me I'd be fine. Tell him I liked that he committed to keeping his beard. It looked nice.

"How are you, Sean?" I managed to say. He shrugged and tried to hide the glitter in his eyes, but I had already seen it. I had not seen him cry before.

"I'm fine. Still haven't killed anyone, so good."

"I see your humor hasn't suffered one bit."

"How would we survive without humor?" he said, lifting his hands. It was heartbreaking to see them held tight by the handcuffs. I couldn't help but remember the time when we were happy, clueless young teenagers going crazy for one another.

"Safe to say that's what's been keeping you sane?"

Sean chuckled. "I don't know about sane, Brie, but I'm alive. I'm good."

"That'll have to do," I said and let out a saddened smile.

"Fine by me. How are you?" Sean asked and leaned forward.

I sniffled and felt my heart skip. Fifteen years. Fifteen years and he still had that effect on me. Able to just render me speechless and catch me off guard, unaware.

"I like the fresh look. The beard," I said and smiled. Sean laughed.

"Thanks, Brie. Still doesn't answer the question. And..." he dragged his chair forward and got stares from the guards watching, with his face getting serious, "why are you here?"

"I came to see you."

"That's obvious, Brie. Why?"

"You aren't worth seeing?" I didn't know how long I could stall and beat around the bush.

"Cut the shit. Go on."

I rubbed my palms on my lap. They were getting sweaty. I knew I didn't have much time, yet I wasn't talking. Either I was scared of the truth I would find or the one I was going to realize.

"Okay."

"Now we're talking, Brie." He reclined into his chair, backing a grey wall. "Hopefully, it's something interesting."

"You have to be completely honest with me, though," I whispered, hoping the guards weren't watching.

"Well, for me to be able to do that for you, you'd need to speak up, love," he said.

"I need to know the truth."

"About what?"

"That day. Fifteen years ago."

He scoffed at my reply. "Here we go." He snorted as he moved uneasily in his seat. I knew it would be difficult to ask him things relating to why he was incarcerated. But it had to be done.

I took a deep breath. "I got a letter, Sean, from someone that knew me. Someone that knew what happened fifteen years ago."

"Okay. Where do I come in?"

"The person also knew about the dead girl that was found, Sean. And so, I'm asking: Is it you? Is this all your doing?"

The silence that ensued seemed to last for minutes. It felt like we were the only ones in the room, and sound didn't exist, safe for when we spoke. Sean broke the silence with what I felt was a sarcastic laugh, I couldn't tell. He changed so much with every visit. Perhaps he was going crazy.

"You're funny, Brie. I'll give you that," he said.

"What? I'm not joking. Why would you—"

"It must be a joke, right? Come on. This is as outrageous as it is funny. The only interesting thing is there's someone else at play. Someone," he said inquisitively.

"Just look me in the eye now, Sean."

He leaned forward and stared deeply into my eyes. I wanted to look away. It felt like he was reaching into my mind to see through me as though he was searching for something.

"Now tell me that you aren't t-the one d-doing all this, behind the letter and the...the dead girls." I swore in my mind and wondered why I stuttered.

"I am not responsible for the letter nor the dead girls, Gabriella. I did drugs, but I'm no murderer," he said, strongly, eyes locked with mine. I could tell he was a little pissed off. "Yes. I confessed to the dead girl in the woods that day, but even if I were to confess again," he raised his hand, both hands held together by a metal clamp into his skin, "this. This is an alibi."

I placed my hand on the steel table and inhaled deeply.

"Why would you think I'm behind this, Brie?"

I scoffed. "Everything points to you. Do you know about that day in the woods? Things no one else could have known were in that letter. And the dead girl in the hut..."

"Are we forgetting one important thing?" Sean tugged at his prison uniform. "Look around. You're at the prison, love. Are we forgetting that part?"

"No, Sean."

"Then, how do I carry out all these things from my prison cell?"

"I don't know... you could escape and have outside help." I didn't even need to wait for Sean to laugh at me before I regretted saying that. I heard myself. I reeked of desperation.

"Wow, Brie. You think that's what I'd do if I was free for some hours every day?" I could see he was genuinely stung by what I had said.

I clasped my hands and put them on my face. "I don't know what to think. Nothing is clear anymore. I don't...get it."

"Let me guide you, darling. Fifteen years ago..." I sat upright and dropped my hands as he said those words. "Fifteen years ago, who else was there and is alive now?"

"Me and you," I said, looking for the point.

"No..." Sean looked at me and waited patiently to have ideas. They flew into my head.

"No... What are you implying?" My voice rose to a pitch.

"I'm just trying to be logical here, Brie. Look at it. You told me to confess. I ended up here. It's been fifteen years, and now you're telling me about things that have happened. I'm just saying—"

"This doesn't make sense, Sean," I said before he could continue. I did not like where it was going.

"Your turn. Why don't you tell me the truth? What happened that day in the woods, Brie?" Sean stared deep into my eyes. "Why did you tell me to confess to the murder of the girl at the hut that day? Who was she? I don't remember ever meeting her until that day." Sean scrunched his back, his hand resting on the table.

Her name was Veronica Clooney, and I had never met her before that day. I knew there were other Veronica Clooneys. What I never knew was what my stepdad did to them. I'm glad I made it out. If I hadn't, I could've easily ended up like her one day.

"Since we are on the topic, Brie, tell me why you asked me to confess to something I didn't do?" he asked.

I don't know when I began to feel goosebumps on my arms and hoped I didn't look as flushed as I had felt.

Hello, Gabriella. What do you wish for?

My head began to ring, and the invitation to play kept replaying in my head once again. On and on. I could hear Sean call my name and snap his fingers to call my attention, but I couldn't move or respond. It just went on and on.

"Geez, Brie, are you all right?" I heard Sean say, and I looked at my wristwatch. Two minutes left.

"Yeah, I'm fine. Headache." I cupped my forehead in my palm sympathetically.

"Hmm," Sean muttered, looking, obviously unimpressed by my final actions. He always knew it when something was wrong; a touch prison hadn't taken that away from him yet. I hoped it would have.

"You should take care of yourself." I smiled.

"I should also say the same. You're not looking bad." He smiled as I reached for my bag.

"Thanks, I'm stressed by the investigations and all such things, but I'm fine." He looked away, and my heart turned sour. He had the same look when I told him to confess to the killing. I told him to take care of the new beard.

"I will, boss." He chuckled, though I could see a corner of his lips twist to the side. The guard came and informed us that time was up. As always, I waited for the guard to escort him inside, watched him walk, took in his physique, and wondered how different things could have been if that day in the woods had never happened.

CHAPTER TEN

Brie

The sound of iron clanging pierced my ears as the gate closed and made my heart jump, and my skin shudders as I walked out of the secure facility.

He said it wasn't him.

I got into my car. The seat was warm, though it felt hot on my skin. I reached for the steering wheel; my hand clammy. A sudden vibration from my phone caused my hand to jerk. I picked up my phone, and the caller ID showed my mum.

"Lily," I said, as she liked to be fondly called. "Sorry, I forgot to call about the foodstuff you sent me."

"That's unlike you, Brie"

I knew her words held sarcasm. I had a busy life as a journalist, and it was hard to keep up with some stuff at times; like: "I forgot."

"Yes, you did, Brie"

Her voice over the phone quivered like she had been crying. It happened every time she thought about my stepdad. I nearly forgot it was the day. My dad died from a hiking accident when I was a baby, and my mum married Daniel, the man I had come to call dad. The alarm on my phone buzzed. It was the eighth of March. The day my stepdad didn't come back home. The day that would make my mum miserable forever.

I ran several words through my mind, looking for the right thing to say. For a journalist, it shouldn't be that hard, right? It came to me eventually.

"It's today, right?"

"Yes, Brie. You know this isn't one of your games," she said. I understood she was sad, but her words were spiteful. I tried to come up with something else to say, but Lily's words replayed.

It reminded me of the stranger's words: "What's your wish, Gabriella?" His words, like a rhyme to the one from fifteen years ago; though Daniel said:

"Hello, Gabriella. What do you wish for?"

"Brie, do you know?" Her words jarred me like the alarm on my phone. "Know what?" I asked. Her breath towered through the line, and I knew she was crying without seeing her. She cried a lot after Daniel left. I left Denton Falls to put the incident behind me but also to hold onto my sanity. To watch her cry over that bastard every day was something I couldn't stand.

"Do you know if he had his inhaler?" she asked.

I ran my eyes for a red sweater on my back seat. One I wore when I arrived at Calitain. I tried to imagine the silver inhaler with a green top, the one Daniel had when he had trouble breathing because he was asthmatic.

"You know he usually forgot to carry it with him, but I checked the house, and it wasn't there." Lily coughed after the words.

Then I thought of the taunting words, envelope, and coordinates that led me to this gruesome sight far too different from his. Yes, the rue flower was the same, but he kept his promise. This wasn't him, but was this nightmare hiding in the shadows? My mouth felt dry. My mum's question was rhetorical. I lied to her, for her. She couldn't take the truth. I lied for her husband, it was best his truth remained unknown. Sean lied to me because of a secret I held over him.

"I will call you back, Mum." I hung up the call.

I dialed Clarissa's number, and over the phone, her voice was breathy, she had to be working out as usual. My boss was what I called a wellness geek: she ate the right thing, lived right, and kept her youthful figure at forty-five.

"There you are, I was worried sick after you left with these numbers. I called Charles, and he said you left some hours ago with the latest info. Called your number, but no response."

"Sorry, I..." I began, but she had known enough about me, and I wasn't going to disclose everything again, especially about Sean. "I was a bit busy researching information on the story."

"What did you find? Anything that could help?" she asked.

"It's still the same information I have. Anyway, the numbers are coordinates, and I'm heading there."

"There? Where?" she asked like I was a child heading out without permission.

"To wherever it takes me, Clarissa."

"By yourself. No, Brie, take Jah with you."

Jah was one of Adam's dogs, a character who was quite disloyal to their fellow journalists. If he got the chance, he would steal my work and make it his own. This was an exclusive news story. It was mine to tell.

"No, Clarissa, I'm good."

Clarissa was a go-getter when it came to news stories. As long as it was newsworthy material, she always taught me not to grow emotionally attached to it, but to see the event which had to be told as just a story. However, at this moment, I sensed she was afraid for me, but I was a survivor, and the story had to be told.

"What's going on?" I asked.

I could hear her take a few breaths into the phone. "You know, Brie, after you told me about your encounter and the ordeal with this scary psychopath, you got me worried. Especially when you mentioned that he recently contacted you."

"I'm going to be okay, Clarissa. I have my Taser," I joked, though the nerves around my neck tingled. I patted my jacket, just to be sure I had my Taser. As a crime reporter, I took it everywhere, you never knew when it could come in handy. I could hear her continue over the phone about me running away if I sensed anything strange at the place, so I replied: "OK, Clarissa. I have texted you the coordinates. If you don't hear from me in, let's say, two hours, then send the police to the coordinates."

My hand felt a bump around the breast pocket of the sweater and the shape of the silver and green inhaler came into my mind. His voice, like a magnetic force, pulled me to a memory of that day.

March 8th, 2007, Denton Falls

His shaky voice was like a four-year-old crying to his mum for candy, and the gruesome tone of his own was gone.

"Well, Daniel, why play with dust, when you are allergic to it?"

"Brie, let me have my inhaler,"

Daniel begged, his face on that day grimed with hope. I was sure these girls begged too. They had the same expectation he wore over his face when death knocked on their door. He never listened to them. I guess, he was human, after all. He wasn't above death.

"Gabriella," he repeated, "let me have my inhaler."

You promised
You promised
On the petals of our love
You vowed to never shed another blood
Yet, you lied again
Here, I stand
On the broken vows, you made
Soiled by an innocent blood
You lied yet again

CHAPTER ELEVEN

Detective Anita

This case had been like a bone stuck in my throat, like a barbecue gone wrong. A stack of books in front of me, my Connect.com page open, and on it several searches:

Rue flower

Meaning of rue flower

The symbolism of the rue flower

I leaned over the books, and it felt as if they mocked me. I couldn't find any information that helped the case. The sick bastard must be somewhere laughing at me, turning me from a prolific detective to a fool. I flipped open yet another page of one of the books.

Penitence, indignation, long-lasting suffering, sin.

What does all this mean?

"Eve."

The name found its way into my thoughts like lightning. Though the killing began last year, they were like the case from fifteen years ago. Why didn't the three victims cross my mind? Was it because I ruled them out because Sean was imprisoned? The other two—I should have checked on their whereabouts after all...

I ran my hands through my loosely tied hair and thought of my visit to Eve. Before my transfer from Denton Falls, I paid a visit to her, and from what I saw, she was very disoriented about time, place, and situation. When she gave her statement at the police station after the three of them were found in the woods, her answers to the situation, place, and people were different from the ones the unrecognizable Eve gave us at the psych ward. How did she change overnight into that girl? Were the three of them lying to protect one another, then who? Or was her trauma a delayed process? Why did I not ask these questions?

I sighed at my mistake, probably because it took a while for me to place it as the work of a copycat instead of the first culprit. Sean locked in prison must have thrown me off.

I ran my eyes for the clock. The said informant placed Brie Owen at the address tomorrow. My phone buzzed, and on the screen, the name Darwin came on.

"Hey," I answered, the call placed into the speaker.

"About your case, you aren't going to like this but..." I could hear a sharp sound buzzing in the distance. He must be in his car, I thought. "Detective Anita, when you talked about the three victims of the case fifteen years ago, I reached out to some of my informants, and one of them reported back to me with something interesting."

Interesting was an understatement when it came to this mouse and cat chase game.

"Intrigue me." I placed my two hands over my waist.

"It's about Eve..." He began

"Okay?"

I watched the time on my computer, switch from seconds into minutes "How about her?"

His pause was so deafening that I wanted to scream into my phone: 'Darwin, spit it out.' I was losing my last patience with this case. "She escaped the psych ward in June 2020."

"Escaped? During winter?" I ran my hand once again through my hair, then glanced at my laptop, today was 22 June 2022.

"Yes, according to my informant. One of the nurses misplaced or got her badge stolen or something, and by the time they realized, Eve was gone."

"Was there an alert for her?"

"Yeah, but she wasn't found, and for a small town like Denton Falls, some people believed she couldn't have survived out there with no help."

For a small town, such as Denton Falls, vast water and land surrounded it; people lived off fishing and farming. To its west, was Mystric (a city of technology) and to its north: was Calitain (a city of art and fashion. Traveling between these cities was hard, especially in the winter season.

"But she could, have found a way..." I thought out loud.

"Found a way?" His voice echoed into the distance. My mind pondered over the information. Why didn't I think of this before?

Though water surrounded it, traveling between both cities was possible. If Eve found a fisherman to take her toward the seashore, then she took a bus to one of these cities.

I bit my lips, afraid of the truth that lingered on them. I ran my eyes for the wall, the address on it, like an irresistible truth. She had been gone from Denton Falls for the past two years.

"Are you there, Detective?"

I put the pieces together, and though the picture and its frame were still apart, something was coming together. A picture perfect for the wall. Eve was either in Mystric, the closest city to Denton Falls or, I swallowed hard, then took a deep breath, she was in Calitain. How could I have missed this?

"Are you there?" he repeated.

"Thank you, Darwin. This was helpful."

"I'm glad it was."

Chaos filled my mind as the puzzle began to form into a picture: the books with the rue flower, pictures of the victims, ligature marks on the recent victims, and no blood found at the scene. A close look at Veronica Clooney's body. Ligature marks, but blood stains around the neck.

I placed my hand over the table and thought, one is compulsive and the other meticulous, though the same MO. Where are you, Eve, and Gabriella? What are you two hiding?

CHAPTER TWELVE

Brie

An old Cherokee is teaching his grandson about life. "A fight is going on inside me," he said to the boy. "It is a terrible fight, and it is between two wolves. One is evil – he is anger, envy, sorrow, regret, greed, arrogance, self-pity, guilt, resentment, inferiority, lies, false pride, superiority, and ego." He continued, "The other is good – he is joy, peace, love, hope, serenity, humility, kindness, benevolence, empathy, generosity, truth, compassion, and faith. The same fight is going on inside you, and inside every other person, too."

The grandson thought about it for a minute and then asked his grandfather, "Which wolf will win?"

The old Cherokee simply replied, "The one you feed."

I sat in my car for half an hour, staring at the coordinates. My heart was beating fast. I keyed in the coordinates into my GPS, the navigation tabulated the route, and I started the ignition. My leg jerked at the sudden sound of the radio. I could feel the worms under my skin begin to crawl. They had been happening more often since the voice from my nightmare came alive. With the phone call from Lily and the unsettling feeling of something, I couldn't place my finger on what was about to happen. An impending doom, a storm which my now sheltered life would be pulled apart from. I thought of that day after I found Daniel in the woods.

March 8th, 2007, Denton Falls

I sat with mum in a grey-painted room with three brown chairs. The floors under our feet were plastered with a brown rug, and on the table sat a coffee cup in front of the black-haired detective it belonged to. I presumed she was in her late twenties. Her eyes were like arrows. They reached into my soul, searching for the truth I held and swore to take to the grave.

Mum was in her green cardigan; one she had thrown over when she got the call about me from the police. She continuously wept while the detective told her I was lucky to be alive. After all, the girl in the woods was the same age, and the one who took her life away wasn't found.

The detective, my second nemesis, asked me to narrate the incident, one which, without the void, would have told mum the truth. A horrifying one, the man she loved was a monster. Detective Anita was relentless. Though I left Denton Falls to build a new life for myself, it was also for the sake of being away from her. She was like these worms that wouldn't go away—always haunting my daydreams, pleading I tell the truth about that day.

I shook my head, wanting to get away from that gruesome sight. A memory that felt like maggots and would only feed off my fear.

The GPS device did its job and located the place.

The woods...

I pressed the gas down, backed up, and drove into the road, the forest up ahead. I drove fast enough to let driving be my only focus and not have me thinking about a thousand things, but slow enough to still be safe. Eighty miles ahead, the navigator chimed. And I drove on, my anxiety shooting through the roof as I got closer to the location. The navigating device instructed me to make a right turn, and as I did, I knew I was there. I parked my car and left the driver's door slightly ajar in case I needed to make a run for it. One could never be too careful, and with the nature of a journalism job, you might be required to dash at some point.

I hoped I would not have to run for my life.

The front door was open, and I entered. I looked around, and my knees buckled. I staggered to the dining table and sat on one of the chairs. I began to feel beads of sweat gather on my forehead. I kept on muttering, "It can't be," because there was no way it was possible.

I was at home... My things...

I stood up when my feet were stable enough and looked out of the window. My car was still parked outside, and I was still in the woods. So, I didn't randomly teleport, nor I was crazy, seeing visions and hallucinating. I slapped myself and pinched my arm until it turned red. Nothing. It was my house.

The dream catcher from a flea market last summer hung over my bed. The floral decor over my window and the soft plush pillow my chief editor gifted me last Christmas. Everything was just like it was before I left the house this morning. Every belonging of mine, there. Perfectly staged.

I ran my hands through the curtains in my room and sat on my bed. It did not smell like home, and I was convinced it was a replica. Or I had all my things stolen this morning. Even the investigation board I had drawn up, with all the newspaper cuttings and notes. Everything. Down to the last detail.

"Who's home?" I heard from the living room and scurried to the dining area, where in my bag I had a Taser. I saw who the voice came from just as I got to my bag. We stood in silence, not moving an inch. I recognized the woman. She was assigned as the detective to the case of the dead girl.

"Hello, Gabriella," the detective said. "Fancy meeting you here," she said, squinting her eyes as if I was hiding something I didn't yet know about.

Like I was back in the nightmare, his cackle broke through my skin, my world was hit by an earthquake, and everything was about to be shattered. My newly built life was about to be taken away. She had walked in and threatened to make the worms go away. She was my nemesis, the one who saw through my lie that day in the woods. I thought I had left it all behind when I moved away from Denton Falls, but it followed me here. The lie I swore to keep hidden with my being would soon be revealed.

"E-rm, yeah. P-pleasant surprise," I managed to say.

"My oh my, you have grown so much, Gabriella."

Her smile was so wide, like one of the TV actors in a toothpaste ad. The same words the killer said over the phone, I had grown, but the lie remained the same as it was fifteen years ago.

"What are you doing here?" she asked. I wanted to say I was at home, but my nerves were in no mood for a dry joke.

"I-I got a lead. Someone sent the coordinates of this place to me." I needed to stop stammering.

"Mhm, is that so, Brie?"

She called me Brie. I knew she could see right through me, but I couldn't let her uncover the truth. "Yes, ma'am. That's it." I could feel the worms, my hand wet. The face of the girl in the hut, Daniel's face with maniac written all over it. His words, What's your wish, Gabriella?

"I don't assume it's our same friend that gave me a lead that your stepdad would be here?"

What does she know? Does she know the truth about Daniel? His death?

"What?"

"Tell me, Brie, how have the last years been for you? Or at least the last fifteen, that was the last we saw of each other." I wasn't comfortable with how she changed the subject and came closer as she spoke, using her index finger to run along the wall paint and rub the dust off on her pants.

"I have been good, actually, yeah."

The detective chuckled. "You sure?"

"Why wouldn't I be?" I retorted. She smiled.

"Changing your name? Everything good, yeah?"

"Everything is good," I spoke bluntly.

"So, our mutual friend. How generous of him to arrange this meeting for us. Are you ready to tell me the truth and what is going on?" The detective drew out a chair from the dining and sat. She was making herself comfortable. Coming into my house too... then I remembered it wasn't my house.

"I have no idea what you're talking about." I sat as well.

"Ah, but you do, Gabriella. You do. The events of that day."

"I'm very lost," I lied.

She took a deep breath as if she was losing her patience. "Brie, we both know Sean didn't do it, but you know who did. You know who our friend is."

My replica room became small and stuffy. The worms under my skin crawled. Beads of sweat returned to my forehead, my palms were soaked. I tried to hide my flustering from the detective, but the smug smile on her face made me know I didn't do well.

"Ma'am, I don't know who is behind t-this." The words came out of my mouth, and I did not even believe them. The detective didn't either.

"But yet you stutter. You don't seem confident in what you're saying."

I couldn't hold it back anymore. My bones were aching, my head felt like it was about to explode. I was done playing dumb. "Because I'm scared! This is a replica of my home. My home! I do not—"

She got up. "You know why," she interrupted. The chair scraped the floor. "Let me help you, Brie. No need to protect him again. I can keep you safe." She spoke with a pleading tone. How did she know the suspect was a he?

"I am serious. I want to find who did this too."

"Brie." The detective put her hand on her face. She was beginning to lose her patience. "This person gave you away. Why are you protecting him?"

I didn't know what she meant by her last words, but I knew nothing. If I were to think about the number of people who hated me and would do this, the list was going to be a long one. After all, I was a crime reporter.

"I told you what I know, ma'am. I swear," I said as I felt my hands tremor.

"You were there that day. The girl was found here, in the woods. You pointed at Sean as the killer, but you and I know the truth. You convinced him to confess. And for some reason, you always turn up where the dead bodies are, yet you refuse to cooperate with me."

She looked at me and brought out a pair of handcuffs. I kept my face of defiance because I felt this was outrageous.

"And speaking of Sean, I had an interesting phone call this evening about Eve. Where is she?" She wasn't asking anymore. She was demanding an answer.

A visit from my third nemesis. One with a gift of indignation. Was she back? The last time I saw her was in the woods, she was bewildered at the truth that Daniel had killed another young girl of our age. The reality of that morning was like a nightmare to us. My actions

... towards the truth, her disdain, and an oath of retribution.

"I have nothing else to say to help your investigation," I said softly, without raising my head.

"You've left me with no option here, Brie. I'm placing you under arrest. Get up and turn around."

"Why am I under arrest when I arrived at the scene just minutes before you did?" I said, raising my eyebrows.

She flinched like there was something in her eyes. Tapped on a walkie strapped over her pant hip.

Sirens from police vehicles and ambulances became louder, and I tried to look around to see what was happening. The detective was frantically making a phone call, and I wondered what had happened. Was there another body? Two other officers rushed into the room, and one of them whispered something into her ear. She walked away, and I followed.

Thoughts ran down my mind. I wished I knew who was behind this, who could make a replica of my home. Who was behind the killings? The detective led me outside and in front of a parked car. The other officer gestured, and I followed.

Chills ran down my damp hands. I ran my hands around my neck and pinched my skin. I wanted someone to wake me up from this nightmare. My chest felt tight, and I couldn't breathe. I stopped walking when I saw it. From the distance, I could see the body of the victim. Just like the other victims, posed in a fetal position.

A flash of the face of the girl in the hut was back. Like a nightmare whilst I was awake, it haunted me. Her pale skin and black hair. Her body was in a pool of blood. Daniel's soiled hands and maniac face as he laughed. His face was like a jester, it mocked me. I had seen these gruesome scenes and victims before. They vividly played in my mind evening. An unsettling feeling seemed new and utterly unknown.

Yet another painful memory was added. The pain took over my whole body, my knees to the floor: the scene of that day replayed. I had gone into the woods, and on my arrival, Sean had dozed off. This had happened before. He was like another person when on drugs, and at times he didn't remember what he did when he was high. This made things easy for me that day. Sean had to be the murderer.

I had to protect Daniel, the man my mum loved so much. The stranger I lived with, though I called him dad. He frequented that hut too. "Do you know there is a hut out there in the woods, where peace abides?" Daniel asked me one morning while he walked me to school. His words were like a poet reciting a poem to an unenthusiastic crowd. His eyes dulled with pain.

"What?" I asked, but silence followed until this day.

At one point, I was curious as to why he told me about it, then lost the curiosity since the secret he revealed worked in my favour. I will never know why he told me about it. Was it because he was tired of hearing mum scold me about Sean? Or he never thought I had the courage in me to get there? Was he luring me there? Had he always planned this?

Every time we went there, we never ran into Daniel because he was a truck driver who was often out of town. On that day, he was out of town, or so I thought, until I shivered at the scene of Sean bent against the kitchen cabinet, my stepdad standing over a young girl, one I think was about the same age as I was at that time. His hands were covered with blood.

"I had to do it. He made me do it."

Yes, my stepdad was diagnosed with psychosis earlier. The doctor said that he hallucinated a lot. It was serious without any treatment: tactile, gustatory, olfactory, and auditory consequences, yet his medications always ended up in our toilet bowl. He said whenever he took these medications, he wasn't himself.

That was our little secret.

I never told mum about that. The gruesome murders had begun in Denton Falls, and I thought they ended after he vowed, but to my dismay, the nightmare followed me until this day in this new city called Calitain.

I was back into the replica. I hadn't noticed until now. Everything was here but the quilt, the one with the fernlike leaves and small, green, yellowish petals. A quilt with an ornamented-rue flower.

His echoing voice spiraled into my consciousness.

"Hello, Gabriella. What do you wish for?"

Was he back?

There was no way this was Daniel.

My stepdad was dead.

He died fifteen years ago.

I killed him.

YOU LIED FOR ME

Except

Chapter II
Brie

The harsh bite of the wind slapped across my face, and I shuddered in response, not just from the wind but the chaos I stood amidst. From my peripheral vision, I could see my car, which was still parked as I had left. A few cops stood scattered around the area, conversing with each other in hushed tones. They weren't whispering, and I only heard it as such because of how dissociated I was from reality.

The trees cast eerie shadows on the ground, intensifying the chills that rippled across my skin. Fallen leaves littered the ground, and crushing sounds were occasionally heard when an officer stepped on dry leaves. I remained fixated on the spot; my body was unwilling to move, and my eyes stayed glued to the dead body, sprawled on the ground in the distance.

My brain refused to process what was happening. The longer I stared, the more confused I got. My guts twisted on my insides, causing my stomach to churn. Everything seemed distant, quite like I was disconnected from the environment. The voices around me blended into a distant, aching symphony, peeling into my skin. I felt an arm pull me by the shoulder, and I blindly followed until we stopped by a police car.

Now, I was much closer to the dead girl's corpse and was able to see a bit more clearly. It was a horrid sight, and as much as I wanted to, I couldn't peel my eyes away. I shuddered again as the wind hit against my skin. The rustling of leaves filled the atmosphere and drowned my internal chaos, but it didn't change the fact that there was a dead girl just a few feet away from me.

My senses heightened, and I scanned the area, desperately searching for Anita, who had pulled me out here. I found her leaning on the car's bonnet, whispering something to a man in a white laboratory coat. I desperately wanted to ask for help and what was happening, but everybody was in their business, and nobody paid me any mind. I wondered how long it would be before they took me out of here. I was getting suffocated, and I had no idea what to do.

My uncomfortable stance and the feeling of cold metal around my wrist reminded me that I was still cuffed. Did she know about Daniel, or did she just arrest me based on suspicion? How were the coordinates connected to Daniel and then the recent murders?

This was my first time being cuffed, and it was an uncomfortable experience as I tried to remain stable while knowing that my hands were bound. I took a deep breath in an attempt to maintain my composure and not lose my mind. The ground beneath my feet barely held my weight as my legs weakened. I tried to distract myself from looking at the body, but despite how hard I tried, my eyes found their way back, and I lingered longer than I would have wanted.

Her hair was sprawled out on the ground above her head, and both hands were on her chest. There was no life in that little body, and it made my skin crawl. I tried to distract myself by focusing on everything else. The smell of wet leaves and dry soil filled my senses and clouded my reasoning. I had to be dreaming - this wasn't real. Although I wanted that to be true, it wasn't. I was still here, in the middle of the woods, my hands cuffed behind my back and my eyes planted on a dead body - again.

It wasn't the first time I was witnessing a dead body, nor was it my second, and it didn't get any better. My response was still the same - shock. It was not like I believed one could get used to seeing dead bodies.

As I stood there, a memory of the past was somehow pushed back, out of the corners of my mind, where it lay buried. It was almost as if I was relieving the nightmare all over again.

I tried to move, but my feet wouldn't budge. My eyes were brimming, and I felt a tear drop hit my cheek. The voices around me became louder and louder, and I desperately longed to cover my ears with my hand, but I couldn't due to my present condition. So, I stayed there and accepted everything as it came.

The new life I had created for myself seemed to have turned a full circle, returning me to the scene I ran from fifteen years ago. Now, I remembered it, clear as day. It was like I was existing at two separate times at once. I was here, staring at this dead girl, and I was also staring at Daniel from fifteen years ago. The image was still ingrained in my memory and stuck to me like a tattoo. It was a stark imagery of a painting by Francisco Goya's Saturn Devouring his Son. The years that had passed meant nothing right now. The scene of myself at the hut that day was too vivid to forget.

Despite the windy atmosphere, I felt beads of sweat break and roll down the side of my face. I couldn't wipe it off, so I let it run. I was panicking but had to keep my composure.

I frantically looked around again, desperate to see if anybody else understood what was happening in my head. Maybe I was wrong, and the cops were used to seeing dead bodies. They didn't seem too fazed, or that was what I thought.

Before my eyes trailed back to the body and caught Anita's, staring right at me. My nemesis. Did she know? Could she see through me? I looked away quickly, just in case she could tell from my body language. Just in case she could see my fear and understand why it was. She was a detective with great skill and experience, so it wouldn't be a surprise if she could. Her stares were intentional.

As I looked back at the body, the story replayed in my head, the bedtime story my mother told me all those years ago about the beast, which, to my surprise, wasn't a story but a real-life tale from which I barely escaped.

I could instantly feel my sweaty wrists against the handcuffs, and I didn't try wriggling my way out. I was not trying to raise any more suspicions, so I stood there, waiting for an order from anyone. The buildup in my stomach seemed to have reached its peak as I struggled to keep myself from retching the contents of my stomach onto the ground. There was no way I could get used to this.

I tried hard to ignore the burning question in my mind. I dreaded the answer. Was Daniel still alive, somehow? It couldn't be. Was it possible that he had somehow escaped death and murdered this girl to torture me some more? My stepfather was dead, and only I knew that. He was a monster who killed the innocent. If that was the truth, then it was working because it felt like I was watching him kill the victim fifteen years ago. I didn't know what to believe, and I felt helpless. I couldn't ask anyone or talk to them about how I felt. I had to somehow keep my thoughts from spilling out of my mouth, just like I had been doing all these years.

I took a deep breath and shut my eyes in a bid to connect to the environment, leaving all my indignation out of my mind. It seemed to work for a few seconds, but that was about the extent of it - just a few seconds. There was nothing else I could do. The memory replayed in my mind as I witnessed it for the first time. Daniel's hands were covered in blood while his victim lay lifeless before him. I saw it. I saw everything, and it haunted me to this very day. It couldn't be that he was alive. Maybe this was just a huge coincidence. I tried to make myself believe that, but the stare I felt boring into my back told me otherwise. Detective Anita was still here, I was still here, the cops were still here, and the corpse...it was still here.

I balled my hands into fists behind me, trying vainly to reduce the moisture. It was an uncomfortable situation.

The atmosphere was gloomy due to the rain that had fallen earlier. The trees swayed noisily. I could hear everything. I heard the slow and calculated footsteps approaching me from behind. The faint smell of lavender became stronger as the footsteps approached. I felt her tap on my shoulder, and I inhaled sharply. Anita was my nemesis, and it didn't look like she would stop until she got something from me.

"Get in the car," she said sharply.

Chapter III
Anita

I watched Brie climb into the car's back seat, taking nervous glances around the area. I knew arresting her would come back to bite me, but she didn't give me any choice. Sooner or later, I would have to release her, but right now, I had to get something from her - anything at all. She had grown up so much since the last time I saw her, but the fact that she was here quickly put all those years behind me. A change of name and some growth didn't change the fact that she was still the same Gabrielle I knew and was still keeping things from me.

Seated in the car, she stared ahead. Her empty stare seemed to hold a lot. I knew she had something on her. She knew something that the rest of us didn't. It could not have been a coincidence that she appeared right where I was. Brie knew something I didn't, and she was adamant. I had to get her to talk before I lost custody of her.

My shoes felt uncomfortable on my feet, and I kicked my legs forward to get rid of the sting.

I had seen many dead bodies during the many years of doing my job, but this particular one seemed out of place. It was a bit too timely to be a coincidence. I didn't believe in coincidences; I believed in perfectly plotted crimes, and this had to be one of them.

My time with Brie was ticking, and I still needed to get her interrogated. I needed to know what it was that she knew. This body seemed to have appeared from nowhere, and it was my job to figure it out. One last look at Brie, and I was convinced she was not planning to run away or do anything questionable, so I exhaled.

I took calculated steps toward the body and crouched down beside it. I had an adrenaline rush, not from witnessing a dead body but from seeing what lay inside it. It made sense to me as everything started falling into place. The dots seemed easy to connect, but it still didn't give me enough answers. The only thing I was able to figure out was the connection to this murder.

I unstrapped my camera from around my neck and turned it on. I focused it on the body, making sure also to capture what lay beside it - a yellow rue flower. After taking multiple shots, I replaced the camera on my neck and examined the body.

There were no strangulation marks or defensive wounds. It was like she knew the killer or just couldn't fight back. As the pathologist had mentioned to me, there were also no needle marks indicating any medication had been introduced into the victim through her veins.

I stood straight and walked around, making mental notes of the questions I would ask Gabrielle.

This case was similar to the Rue killer case from fifteen years ago in Denton Falls. I would easily say it was another one of those cases that never ended. The Rue killer was still out there, whoever they were, and they wanted to tell us they were back.

I felt a little lightheaded at the thought of it. This was a case I picked up again since it was never fully solved, and just around this period, when I reopened the file, I came across another one. I stood there for a few more minutes, gloved hands on my waist, processing what I witnessed. I felt my head throbbing lightly, and I blinked back in an attempt to make it go away.

I knew I shouldn't have arrested Brie, but she was my only link to solving this case, as this was a remarkably similar murder, and she was there both times. I had my suspicions based on the fact that this was a completely different city. This wasn't Denton Falls but Calitain, a much bigger city. It was most certainly not a coincidence.

The text I received from an anonymous person directing me to this place and telling me that Daniel Caravan, Brie's stepfather, would be there was enough to put me on my toes. Why would anyone tip me like that? I thought it was odd, but I was determined to find Daniel, so I followed their instructions. However, I wasn't sure what or who I would be meeting. I came here because of that reason, and to my surprise, I saw Brie here instead on arrival. Someone carefully planned this, and it had to be someone who was also connected to this murder, somehow. I wasn't sure, but Brie was my only lead, and I had many questions for her.

This place was in the woods, far from town, so this person had carefully planned the meeting between Brie and me. I straightened out my uniform, looking around for any other leads. Why did they want me to meet Brie?

In all my years of experience, I've had multiple cases, but this particular one stuck out as odd. I never understood why the killer always kept rue flowers beside his victims. I believed it was for identity and easy linking, but why would they want everybody to know who they were if they were in hiding?

Fifteen years ago, Brie's mother had told me to help her find her husband, Daniel Caravan, who she suspected would be here in Calitain, and the text I received linked me to this place with the assurance that he would be here, and I'd finally got my answers. But seeing Brie here instead only gave me even more questions. What was she hiding, and why? Why was she trying to protect the Rue killer?

All these years, I had held off from fulfilling my promise to her mother until now, and it seemed like I was being watched and monitored. Whoever sent the message to me knew that I was looking for him, which disturbed me even more.

Since this was the case, it had to be no different from Brie's. She mentioned that someone gave her the coordinates to this place, and if she was telling the truth, she had to be involved with the case somehow.

Instead of trying to protect this person, I would rather she opened up to me and helped me solve this faster. I had my suspicions, but without her statement, it was baseless. I had to be sure of everything, which would make my work easy. Now we had another body on our hands and the killer on the loose. I needed to interrogate Brie as soon as possible. I had no time to waste. I didn't want to give the killer time to kill more innocent people and go scot-free. I was not about to sit back and watch him have his way like he did fifteen years ago. This was the first, and I needed to ensure it would be the last.

I walked around for a few minutes, but the ground was covered in leaves and rocks, and nothing in particular stood out. Rubbing my forehead, I sighed in frustration. He needed to be found and stopped in time because I knew this would not be his last victim. If only Brie would cooperate.

Minutes later, we were on our way back to the station. Another van had come to retrieve the body while we left in the car. So far, Brie hadn't said a word except her occasional mumbling under her breath. If anything, she looked confused and lost. I could also sense her fear. I stared ahead as the questions formed in my head. In just a few minutes, I would get my answers from Brie. I only hoped she would cooperate with me.

Chapter IV
Brie

Brie, I was getting impatient and annoyed at the fact that she refused to budge and leave me alone. We had been here for about fifteen minutes already, and my head was hurting. I couldn't complain; I just had to play it off.

She kept asking the same question, and my reply was the same. I tried to avoid explaining too much to avoid accidentally revealing my secret. It was bad enough that she was convinced I had a secret; I wouldn't do her the favor of saying it. The glass of water on the table was nearly empty, and I constantly drank from it whenever I got nervous. I grabbed it with my free hand and took one more gulp as my other hand was cuffed to the table.

"I know nothing about it. I've said this several times already. I'm just as surprised as you are, detective." It was a struggle trying to maintain a neutral tone and not give off any signs of rage. I knew they were monitoring me closely, waiting for me to slip.

Anita's gaze was firm as her eyes held mine. She was seated across from me at the other end of this large table. The interrogation room was simple - a large rectangular table with two chairs on both ends. There was a large, one-sided mirror on the wall, and I knew cops were on the other side, watching my every move.

"I told you I received a coordinate which led me there, just like you received a message. I was just as surprised as you are right now. It didn't make sense to me, either." I tried to convince her, but the lack of any expression on her face told me that she was not very convinced and that I would have to do a better job. "Fifteen years ago, detective, I was unconscious during the whole ordeal and didn't wake up until you arrived," I finished, hoping she would believe me now. Even I didn't have too much faith in my words.

"And by coincidence, do you happen to be involved in the same case now?" Her voice gave off a hint of sarcasm, sending me on edge. She was adamant. "Your chief editor told us you were covering a news story about the Rue killer," she gave me a skeptical look, narrowing her eyes to slits. I knew I had to be careful with my words and body language. She had so much experience, and I was just one of the many people she had interrogated over the years.

"Detective," I started, keeping my tone neutral, devoid of emotion. " I didn't even know about the Rue killer case until my chief editor called me three days ago and asked me to cover the news story, which was already on the television, by the way. I also had to interview Dave, one of the witnesses, who told me he was so scared that he couldn't even help the victim even though he saw her brown eyes while she died."

"So, do you mean to tell me that you didn't know that your stepfather was to come to this address? Your mum asked me to look for your stepfather while I was being transferred, and during my search, I received a message that Daniel Caravan would be at that address, which was why I went there. But guess what?" She paused, holding my eyes with a look of accusation. "To my surprise, you were there instead. Now, how do you explain that to me?" her lips curled up slightly, and I felt intimidated. Anita was my nemesis; she wouldn't leave me alone.

I could feel my right hand get greasy on the table, but I didn't pay attention. At this point, it seemed like she would use the smallest bit of suspicion against me. The way she composed herself told me that she would not let me go very easily. She looked determined to get something out of me. Her tone was firm. She knew what she wanted to hear, and it was up to me to keep what I knew to myself.

I watched her as she sat up, adjusting her posture and taking a gulp of her water. Her black hair was in a bun, with a few strands framing her face. She replaced the now empty glass on the table and clasped her hands together on the table.

"So apart from the victims, which I know you know more about but aren't disclosing, where is your stepfather? Maybe you can answer that one for me, Brie," she asked, cocking her head to the side. She seemed to have carefully practiced what to ask and had the upper hand, as all her questions left me unaware.

I swallowed hard. She knew exactly what she was doing. I searched my brain for the perfect response, but none was forthcoming. The pressure I felt was gradually building up, and I feared I would say something I should not have. Her aura was intimidating. I felt a bead of sweat form on my forehead as I got even more nervous.

The truth was that I had no idea where Daniel was. The last time I saw him, he was lifeless, and if he somehow was able to come back to life, then I was just as clueless as she was. But notwithstanding, I couldn't disclose any of that to her. If I did, all the work I put into creating a new life for myself would go down the drain. I would be arrested.

Daniel was a monster who didn't deserve to live, and what I did should have been considered heroic, but unfortunately, it wasn't. I still had to hide everything, so I kept my stare and didn't say a word, hoping she would get tired and release me.

The silence loomed between us, filling the room with unimaginable tension. I directed my gaze down to the table, as staring at her did no good. I didn't know what I was waiting for, but if she was waiting for me to say something, we would be here for a long time.

I tapped my foot against the ground as anxiety washed over me. I couldn't help but think about the latest victim. Was Daniel truly alive? Was my stepfather back? I shut my eyes briefly, trying to block out that thought. If he was, then I was in danger. Many people were.

Whoever was behind that murder? It also had to be the same person who sent the coordinates to me. I still had not gotten over the fact that there was a whole replica of my house. The memory caused me to shudder in my seat. Who was behind all of these? I had so many questions and zero answers. My mind was filled up, and I felt defeated.

I knew it was getting late, and I did not intend to sleep in jail. I silently prayed for a miracle to get me out of here soon. I feared that if I stayed here for too long, I would reveal things to her, which would put me in trouble.

All I wanted was to put this behind me and continue living my regular life here in Calitain. I would have never imagined that the killer would come out of Denton Falls all the way to Calitain. This was my escape city, but now it was not anymore.

As if on cue, the stern voice of a man outside the interrogation room drew our attention, causing the detective to stand up abruptly and walk towards the door. The man stood outside, but I could hear their conversation.

"Sir," she greeted him. He sounded aggravated, yelling at her.

"When I got a call from Chief Marcela, telling me that one of my team members had arrested a civilian without a cause, you could imagine my surprise," I heard him speak. "Why would you think of arresting a journalist without cause?" he barked. "The people have already been stating that the police are using force and violence in the public, and now you just put handcuffs on a journalist. What reputation are you trying to give to us?"

"But sir," Anita tried to say something but was interrupted by the man, who, by now, I had concluded was her boss. "No buts. Release her at once," he ordered, his voice commanding.

"Yes, sir," I heaved a sigh of relief as I was grateful. The tension in the room disappeared quickly. I was going to be out of here in a matter of minutes. Anita walked back into the room, wearing an unpleasant expression. She was not the most excited about what she was about to do. She unhooked the key to the cuffs from her trousers and un-cuffed me.

Don't miss out!

Visit the website below and you can sign up to receive emails whenever Zee David publishes a new book. There's no charge and no obligation.

https://books2read.com/r/B-A-VIWU-BBBCC

BOOKS 2 READ

Connecting independent readers to independent writers.

Did you love *I Lied For You*? Then you should read *Her Web Of Lies*[1] by Zee David!

[2]

A fire.An informant.

Five death

Conclusive evidence.

Will Brie trust the evidence or listen to her informant

Was the fire an accident- or was there, a foul play?

Her web of lies is the third in the mystery novella: Brie Owen series.

1. https://books2read.com/u/3R5NXx

2. https://books2read.com/u/3R5NXx

www.ingramcontent.com/pod-product-compliance
Ingram Content Group UK Ltd.
Pitfield, Milton Keynes, MK11 3LW, UK
UKHW040031200726
13854UKWH00001B/462

9 798215 057292